Children and Fools

ERICH FRIED

Children and Fools

Translated by
Martin Chalmers

Translators note: I should like to thank Denise Riley for help
with the verses. M.C.

This translation received financial support from the
Commission of the European Communities, Brussels

Library of Congress Catalog Card Number: 92-60139

British Library Cataloguing in Publication Data
Fried, Erich
  Children and Fools
  I. Title II. Chalmers, Martin
  833.914[FS]
  ISBN 1-85242-211-4

The pieces in this collection are taken from the following books
published by Verlag Klaus Wagenbach, Berlin: *Kinder und
Narren, Fast Alles Mögliche, Das Unmaß aller Dinge*, and *Mitunter
Sogar Lachen*.
Copyright © 1965, 1975, 1982, 1986 by Verlag Klaus
Wagenbach.
Kinder und Narren: Prosa © 1965 by Carl Hanser Verlag,
Munich and Vienna

This collection first published 1992 by
Serpent's Tail, 4 Blackstock Mews, London N4 and
401 West Broadway #2, New York, NY 10012

Translation © 1992 by Serpent's Tail

Typeset in 10/12½ Baskerville by
Contour Typesetters, Southall, London

Printed in Denmark by
Norhaven A/S, Viborg

Contents

Atonement

Yesterday, before going to sleep, I drank up my milk, which as a child I had spilled in anger. I drank it out of the cup with the floral design, and as I emptied it, I saw at the wet gleaming bottom the big red rose, just as my grandmother had always promised. Except that I had never drunk up then, and had finally smashed the cup. This time, however, my grandmother would be satisfied with me, I knew that.

But now, since I've drunk up and seen the bottom, there is much to be done. A great deal has to be made good and some things have to be undone. I was always a little sad after Aunt Erna's death, because I had been cheeky the last time I saw her. But this morning I visited her and apologised, and she was nice again and gave me a sweet as usual.

I also rang up my friend Hans, at the flat where he used to stay. I had neglected him in the end because I was constantly preoccupied with my own problems. I gave him good advice and admitted to him that I had the same doubts as he did. It's almost twenty years ago now, but we're meeting tomorrow during lunch. He laughed and said, never again will he do himself any harm.

Much has still to be put right. With Irene and with my first wife, and — if I can brace myself to do it and can actually discover the overgrown spot — even with my father. But at least things are moving again now! It's worth straightening out these old stories. It's never a waste of time to look people up and settle old misunderstandings once and for all, by simply discussing things with them, openly, just as one should talk to relatives and old friends. I feel happier and more free with every hour that passes, and all at once life is again full of promise and possibilities.

St. George and His Dragon

It is said that St. George came from Cappadocia and killed a dragon, which wanted to devour a beautiful maiden. Legends love simple deeds and recognisable heroes. It is nowhere recorded that St. George loved the dragon.

He had known his dragon ever since childhood, at an age when the volts and twists of jousting beneath the rough-barked or moss-covered trees were more important to him than any reflection on the beauty or deformity, the excellence or wickedness of his play companion. Later too, if thoughts as to the alien nature of his friend occurred to the boy, who was by then wearing his first light armour, he quickly cast them from his mind. He forgot them, just as he did the dismal rows of figures of his strict arithmetic teacher. No, he did not want to add up differences. He preferred to stick to what he and his playmate had in common. They were both spirited and skilful, proficient at the contest — each in his way — and they both loved the ruffled grass and the old lime trees, singed by tongues of fire, beneath which George's comrade had its dwelling. Sometimes George even believed that he recognised in the other's strange outer skin a scaly armour similar to the light, silvery one that he himself wore. He wore it to please his friend, he said to himself; the armour made him harder, more like the other.

George had romped with the dragon ever since childhood, had swung himself up onto its comb, had slipped through its two coils or laughingly evaded claws and blows of the tail in their wrestling bouts. He had also learned to understand the other's language. What sounded to the people, who kept at a safe distance, like hissing and grunting, George understood without any effort. Sometimes it moved him and made him sad, for what the other said was often full of hopeless wisdom.

About this time, however, George did sometimes become uncertain. The dragon really was very different from him. Now and then, on a whim, or perhaps out of despair — George never quite knew which it was — the dragon laid an ambush. Then it could cause more mischief than the worst highway robber. Admittedly it was then sad for days afterwards and could not even be aroused for a game among the trees. It lay listlessly outside its dwelling. Tears dropped from the lower lids of its eyes, which did not shut even when a fly landed first on one, then on the other. And there, where the scaly armour did not quite cover the dragon's face, it was almost as white as the bleached and carefully arranged pyramid of skulls at the edge of the glade, which grew taller year by year. But George sat on a stone, his elbows resting on his knees, his chin in the palm of his hand, and looked helplessly at the dragon, until his head grew dizzy and stupid.

The people said to George that they did not understand how he could pass his time with the repulsive reptile. But George knew more about the reptile than about people. Even small, seemingly unimportant peculiarities, which would perhaps have appeared contemptible or ridiculous to other people, seemed touching and lovable to George — for example, that the dragon was afraid of spiders.

When the mountain of skulls at the edge of the glade grew taller than the road sign — the foot of which was beginning to disappear beneath the skulls that had rolled down — the people were goaded into fury by this interference with their devotions. They called upon George finally to kill the dragon. Yes, he must do it, because he knew its wiles better than anyone else. By that time George had already often wondered whether his dragon was not simply a burden to itself and to the world. All kinds of dark thoughts had occurred to him, but now, when the people called upon him to slay his childhood companion, he shrugged his shoulders and went into the wood. In the thoughts of these people there was only an unrefined mixture of fear and vengefulness; even their just complaint was thereby turned into injustice and a thirst for blood.

George took the few people whom he loved with him to the clearing. He persuaded them not to treat the dragon like a monster. George told himself it was above all necessary to convince his old playmate that it was not completely lonely and forgotten in the wood.

The dragon gave these guests presents of jewellery and beautifully forged weapons, that it was again and again able to find in the tall grass of its forest glade. The visitors promised to return, but even if George, who was forgetful when it came to people, remembered one or other of these arrangements a few weeks later and went into the villages to visit his friends, he met only with hostile glances. The people whom he had known had disappeared. George regretted that. He told himself that the dragon — apart from everything else — must thus always remain lonely and unloved and dependent on him alone.

Finally, when George could bear it no longer, he went alone to his dragon. He had not slept and not eaten for three days. His old playmate could easily have knocked him down.

They stood facing one another in the morning sun. George looked first at the dragon and then at his sword. He was racked by a severe headache and he could hardly keep his eyes open. He would never be able to force himself to do it.

At that moment the dragon must have noticed George's armour, perhaps because of the twinkling of the sun. It was only a light, useless, dress armour, not a jousting suit. But it was brightly polished, and the dragon saw its reflection in each scale. It could see it too in George's broad sword, only there it trembled, because George could hardly keep himself on his feet and his hand was shaking. It occurred to him to ask the dragon for help.

Old books of legends relate of basilisks and dragons, that they burst if a mirror is held in front of them. Apparently their own reflection is fatal to them, which is perhaps also evidence of the sensitivity of which George had always spoken. Or could the dragon no longer bear the expression in George's eyes?

Admittedly, the old legends did not prove to be right. The dragon did not burst. Its hard, horny, armoured skin held firm, but something inside it must have torn or ruptured. The legs buckled; first the hind legs, so that it looked as though the monster were kneeling at the feet of its old play fellow. Then the front legs gave way too.

The people turned up at the edge of the glade, as the dragon was already rolling in the grass, twitching and wheezing. Whether these sounds of pain had any meaning the people did not know. They had never understood the dragon's language. They only saw that George drew his hand across his brow, stepped up to the dragon, quietly nodded several times and then slowly, almost gently, drove his sword into its breast. Only then did he cut off its head.

It is not known whether George said anything afterwards, whether he wept or laughed. Any words would have been drowned out in the jubilation of the crowd. Every hand stretched out and reached for him. The victory celebration began.

There is nothing to relate here of the beautiful maiden who was saved from the dragon. Perhaps she was too unimportant, perhaps too important. One may remain silent about the inessential, about the essential too, especially if no good can come of it any more.

St. George himself is said to have been beheaded many years later in a place far away.

Father of All Things

In this field too, everything was useful and practical. At times when important political decisions had to be taken, but especially before a campaign, the government had to be informed about the morale of its troops. Then the Council of Elders gave its assent, and a hundred prisoners were brought onto the parade ground, captured warriors, though now wearing only a loincloth. A brief command and they were cut down by a hundred soldiers, who as usual had been drawn from various regiments and services.

There followed of course the entry onto the grey lists, that is, the time required for the action was carefully recorded there and then. A few hours later, however, the bodies of the prisoners were brought to the Practising Elder, who could determine the morale of the soldiers in question from the nature, number and depth of the fatal wounds. It was always only a question of fatal wounds, not of course in the case of each individual injury, but certainly in the overall picture of the wounds of each individual prisoner. It did not happen that a prisoner was merely wounded and allowed to live; the morale of the fighting troops had never sunk as low as that.

The greatest care had always to be taken in the conduct of the action, for the Practising Elder was concerned with exact knowledge. He expected conscientious and precise observation of his instructions by everyone, including the prisoners who had to fall in for the action.

The soldiers, whom the Council of Elders detailed to carry out these experiments, were not to be the most spirited of their units, nor the weakest. Also, they each had to possess the usual degree of familiarity with their weapons. At the behest of the Practising

Elder the closest attention was devoted to the weapons themselves, since their length and sharpness, their weight and naturally also their quality always had to be the same. They were not allowed to vary in different actions. The Practising Elder had first of all made clear to the rulers, then also with all due form to the Council of Elders and finally, courteous as he was, even to the representative assembly of the people, that with non-uniform weaponry, varying from action to action, an especially deep cut, which might easily be welcomed as a sign of great pugnacity or resolute patriotism, need mean nothing more than that a particularly sharp or heavy weapon had been involved.

The Practising Elder's much praised welfare work with prisoners was also based on considerations of a similar kind. He placed great value on always having the prisoners fall in for the action in approximately the same condition and temper. For, so he warned, if, for example, they had become weary of life because of particular torments, then some could willingly throw themselves on the swords of their attackers; if, on the other hand, they were fed too well and too much during their captivity, then again the sluggishness of their plump carcasses could give rise to unusual and misleading wounds. So, little by little, the Practising Elder worked out a sound and efficient method of evaluating all the weapons and people involved in the test actions.

The inquest itself was always a difficult task for the Practising Elder, because he was by nature extremely sensitive. Before they were presented to him, the corpses always had to be carefully cleansed of blood and excrement in order to free his sad duty, as he called it, at least of its worst horrors. The kind-heartedness of the Practising Elder was also evident in his insistence on shutting with his own hands the eyes of his dead, in so far as they were still there. He always spoke of *his* dead; he made no use of the official term 'major action remains accrueing'.

Sometimes it was necessary to compare the morale of one unit with that of another. In such cases several hundreds of prisoners had to be subjected to the measures strictly prescribed by the Practising Elder and then examined by him. The Practising Elder considered experiments with smaller groups inexpedient.

He could, it is true, have made his sad duty considerably easier, but he explained that with a smaller group of test prisoners the possibilities of error would be too large and so could no longer be offset by a reliable average. Furthermore, the Practising Elder declared the action with larger groups of prisoners, that is, with these classic hundreds, to be easier to defend morally, since as a result, life was made more difficult for himself, the Practising Elder. Experiments which could not be completed without the infliction of pain could be morally justified only when pain was distributed on both sides. With a smaller number of test prisoners the pain inflicted on them weighed heavier than the torment he suffered through having to examine his dead. This, of course, was an injustice. But the death agony of a group of a hundred was only ten times the death agony of a group of ten. However, his pain in the performance of his sad duty on larger groups of dead increased much more rapidly, the examination of twenty dead already caused him three times as much pain as the examination of ten dead, and with a quantity of a hundred test prisoners his pain, made up of a mixture of sympathy, disgust, horror and so on, was approximately equivalent to the total death agony of that particular hundred. Only this balance, however, granted the action its moral legitimation.

That the Practising Elder always took great care is well known, and, although his statements could in themselves be considered so reliable that any suspicion would appear, at the very least, to be quite inappropriate, there also exists documentary proof that the actions can not at all have consisted of one-sided cruelty, but that the highest human feelings found expression in them and that even the prisoners were able to value the task of the Practising Elder. For preserved among the literary monuments of that time is also the poem of a prisoner, written on the eve of an action and evidently addressed to the Practising Elder himself. It reads:

No longer in the noise of battle,
No longer scourged by fear to the black gall of rage,
To despair at sense and outcome,

No, safely sheltered
In the golden net of certainty,
Like the fish, which no longer defends itself,
If the gods have destined it
To gleam in the bright light on the king's table,
I live for the final meeting with thee, O Practising Elder!

Surely I come to thee as night towards morning,
Providently thou guidest the waning of my being.
It is thou, who faithfully metest out my food and drink,
Thou, who hath ordained my bed:
Not too hard, not too soft,
Who fans the air, the breath of my last days,
Not too frosty and not too hot,
Not too damp nor too dry.
I am consecrated to thy service, O Practising Elder!

Not senselessly, ebbs my blood
Like my brother's blood on field of battle;
No enemy notches my skin
Without thy manifest will,
Not one hair of mine head is harmed,
Without that thou knowest of it.
Thou layest thy warm hands in my cold wounds:
That pains thee longer than me.
Thou takest up the burden, O Practising Elder!

To make the accident of slaughter serve the cause of
    wisdom,
The death of my body the life of thy spirit,
Shalt thou test me,
When I no longer am,
Shalt thou know me
When I no longer know myself,
In the clarity of thy reason and of thy senses,
In the rigour of thy calculations and of thy labour,
In the time after my time, O Practising Elder!

Reading these ancient verses one can scarcely withstand the emotion which threatens to overwhelm one in recognition of how, even so long ago, truly human thought and feeling could soar beyond all seeming enmity, indeed, even beyond death, to an awareness of and passion for the great common task which united the Practising Elder with his dead, the hundred prisoners with those who carried out the action on them. This poem, however, is not only evidence of the truth of the statements and the reasoning of the Practising Elder which have been passed down to us, but, with its words wrung from the profoundest depths of fate, also testifies to the great moral height to which, even then, he was able to raise relations with friend and foe, not, of course, relations in the sense of the malicious rumours about the Practising Elder's alleged passion for corpses. For the people of our age, such proofs and testimonies are as salutary as they are sadly necessary, simply to nip lighthearted arrogance in the bud. For since the days of those old experiments, military technology and research methods have changed considerably and nothing would be easier for us, as remote descendants of the Practising Elder and his first pupils, than to turn up our noses at those old and, in some respects admittedly, obsolete usages. And yet it was precisely the test actions, so often repeated and so carefully recorded in the old chronicles because of their importance to the state, which provided the impetus for almost every branch of our immense contemporary knowledge, not only the initial results, but also the methods and procedures in almost every area of knowledge.

So the Practising Elder's observations on the variation in wounds on cold and hot days led first of all to the determination of the ideal weather for battle and thereby to our superiority and to those decisive victories, to which we, as remote descendants, owe the diffusion and flowering of our culture. Subsequently they led also to new methods in the measurement of air temperature, of atmospheric pressure, of humidity and wind force and thus through meteorology to the foundation of contemporary weather analysis.

Investigations also took place into prisoners' attempts at flight in the short time between the start and conclusion of an action. They arose, because the attempt at flight had, in turn, not been without influence on the form and depth of wounds. These investigations led first of all to the examination of the precise condition of the terrain of action over which the attempts at flight had been undertaken, and beyond that to general scientific research into land and soil. It emerged that evenness or roughness of the ground, surface cover of sand or various plants, even small or very small plants, was not without significant influence on the effectiveness or ineffectiveness of the final attempts at flight of those prisoners. That is already demonstrated by the earliest surviving work of the Practising Elder, on which so many works by later authors are based, the "Great Footsole Inquest". Its motto, "Without tears! Eyes clear! Let their fate not be in vain," is at once scientifically, humanly and poetically significant.

However, recognition of the importance of the condition of the ground subsequently led to a general investigation of the land and soil and of the various grasses and mosses which cover the ground, as well as of the diverse types of rock or kinds of sand and dust. These were the earliest beginnings of our contemporary botany, mineralogy and geology as well as of the military research of escape routes and science of dead ends.

It is also easy to understand that the conditions of light at the time of these actions necessarily exerted considerable influence on the accuracy of the participating soldiers as on flight and pursuit movements. Light measurement and optics, the whole of the contemporary lighting industry and even, as a further consequence, astronomy, developed out of the modest lighting studies embarked upon at that time, since, even then, the Practising Elder was much too thorough simply to neglect the influence of some radiant body placed in the heavens.

Furthermore, the behaviour of the prisoners was dependent on their ability to communicate with one another. Certain modes of behaviour could spread much more quickly in those hundreds that had predominantly monosyllabic languages rather than long-winded languages which consisted of polysyllabic words.

This gave rise to the science of comparative command language as well as to a variety of studies, which later became, in part, the bases of our contemporary ethnology and anthropology and, in part, made possible the invention of time-and thought-saving work and military languages. The value of the actions, and of the Practising Elder's subsequent investigations, for medicine, psychology, the theory of function satisfaction and the science of dead souls — and on the other hand, for the development of probability theory and for the statistical sciences and auxiliary sciences in general as well as for the foundation of a general methodology — are obvious.

But even the apparent human weaknesses of the Practising Elder have not only turned out to be fruitful, but have also simultaneously become an admonition to us not to hastily prejudge attributes of outstanding persons as true weaknesses, even if at first they seem odd to us. So, for example, the inability of the Practising Elder to bear the sight of blood provided the decisive impulse for the discovery of styptic agents, which not only benefit countless patients, but without which today's flourishing mortuary industry would be inconceivable, especially after traffic accidents. Yet more than that, chemistry itself was born then or at least, if one may say so, given its baptism of blood, not least thanks to the constant search of the Practising Elder's assistants for spot-removing liquids, which could spare him the sight of spilled blood, without, however, at the same time causing alterations in the wounds themselves.

The proverbial scrupulousness of the Practising Elder sometimes led to him being forced to spend many hours, even whole days, over a single corpse. To enable him to do so, the foundation stone of today's frozen meat and refrigeration technology was laid, which in turn again forms the physical basis of our promising science of dead souls.

It was much the same in various branches of the humanities. The Practising Elder concluded that the influence of their religion, indeed, even the influence of quite specific laments or tragic songs, was clearly recognisable in the behaviour of prisoners during their decisive final moments. This not only led to the comparative study of religions, but music and poetry for the first time also became objects of comprehensive and systematic research, which helped to found new branches of knowledge, without which, for example, our contemporary limitations theory would be unthinkable. Some even maintain, that our efforts at systematisation in matters of state can originally be traced back to those test actions. The extremely high cost of the actions for those days is said to have given the initial impetus to administrative accountancy and to have finally led, via a detour through so-called political economy, to our comprehensive science of human maintenance and restraint.

Whatever is true in individual cases, it is certain that the blood which ceased to flow long ago, which was shed in the test actions of those far-off days, did not flow in vain for any of us, not even for the functionally satisfied and restricted. It continues to flow through all the veins and arteries of our contemporary culture, which it helped to found and to which it has lent its unique colouring. It is its immortal fluid, its eternally efficacious, eternally circulating life sap.

Miss Gröschel

He took his own life. Well yes, those are words that the inventors of mourning borders and the makers of ribbons for wreaths must have thought up. But now I was really free. Only I could not expect any more money, because the bankruptcy was of course to blame. No bankruptcy, no voluntary death. News of both came by the same post. For me the death of my father meant above all that I could at last give up my so-called studies. I did not have to resit any more examinations just to be allowed to stay in New York. Now a new life could begin in earnest. A death cleanly and neatly separates one period of one's life from the next, almost as in my school days, when I had not yet got out of practice, my fruit knife separated the head from the rump of a fly. Or, to keep in step with the times, almost like a war. It would come soon too. In Europe it had already been going on for almost two years.

Originally I should have gone home, to do my duty, but military service and I, that too was now out of the question. Besides, who had asked me whether I agreed? Neither one side nor the other. I wasn't needed for that anyway. After all, there's never a lack of people who are prepared to do the actual work of slaughter. It's just the same when the job of hangman is advertised, and the applications come pouring in. And also if there should ever be a shortage of workers in the slaughter houses; they would only need to show a colour film of what it's really like. Then they would have enough willing hands, and most would even be ready to pay for it out of their own pockets. At least I was never short of helpers later on. But for me personally it was of no interest.

Actually, at the time I had not yet undertaken anything at

called me a cheeky bug. Now the finger under the bug. Here it is, here it is! I've got it! It's still wriggling. It must certainly be quite wet. I cannot see that it's wet, but only the dear Lord can walk on water and not get wet, and I love the bedbug, but it is not the dear Lord, I know that very well, because to it I am the dear Lord. If it thanks me, it will say, thank God, but it is only a bedbug, it won't thank me. Bugs are ungrateful beasts. But now I put it on the linen cloth, where it crawls itself dry, and I blow on it to make it warm. So. Now it's crawling. A wet trail is left behind on the linen cloth, but not at all yellow or even yellowish. Because whatever is not yellow, but is nevertheless yellow, is called yellowish. I love you, you dear thing, and give your mama and grandmama my regards! We say mama, of course, but we say grandmama because grandmama was already big, when mama was still small; and then, if one is sending them regards, one must speak as grown-ups speak. So: I send both of them my regards, do you understand, cheeky bedbug? My acknowledgement, because I know you now. Bedbugs stink, but nevertheless I still give you a kiss. It doesn't stink at all. I smell only the linen cloth underneath it, which I almost kissed too. And don't let yourself be caught again.

But don't forget: if I'm really left to drown in the lavatory bowl, or if I'm really torn into little pieces in mid-air, then you must come to my funeral. Then all the animals I have saved come to my funeral. And they all are dressed in mourning as in the big poster of the vermin exterminators, on which all the vermin wear mourning too, because they must die with all their loved ones . . .

And all the animals earnestly and solemnly fire three times in the air, like the soldiers on Corpus Christi Day, and weep for me, and their tears flow like the brook in the meadow. And then the bedbugs accompany grandmama home and show her the way, because she really doesn't see very well, and I'm lying in my grave and can no longer tell her when there's a step or a car is coming. But in my grave the worms come and say that I was so kind to the animals, and that's why they don't eat me but only curl round me and warm me, and some worms are bright and shiny, because they are so smooth. They give me light, while others bore little holes out of the grave, so that I have air, as when I lie under the blanket and make a very small round hole for myself under the edge of the blanket, but above the sheet, so that I can breathe again, and so I lie there with my worms like Snow White in her coffin, and Anna shakes her head and says again, "That boy's scared of nothing," and then the girls from the Corpus Christi procession come in their white dresses. They come walking and not flying, because they don't want to make me dizzy. So they have folded up their wings and handed them over to the moths and the naphthalene pellets, which don't hurt, and to the bedbugs, who are praying for me the whole time, and come as walking, not flying, angels. And two of them are Lili and Paula, and they take me by the hand and lead me past the high wall of the park along the whole of Liechtensteinstrasse and up into heaven.

Deliverance

Oh, the great ones, who cover up or despise the true and gild the forgery and then raise a washed and dried index finger and say: Silence is golden!

For not everything that is true can be beautiful and glitter. That which stinks also floats in that which smells, the shit in the urine, the dumpling in the soup, but if you bend down deeper into the pot, without pause, so that the night pot turns into a day and night pot, then you will find everything. Everything: the child's sunken boat, an ocean steamer, and the smell of ripe apples, and the colours — the colours and the reflections — and the drowned bedbugs which grandmama threw into the night pot, because war is war. And one of them is still squirming, and you will stretch out your finger to it even if you feel disgusted. You will stretch out your finger, then it wants your whole hand, but you are a swine. No. You are not a swine, because you love it. What you do not want done to yourself . . .! And if you had fallen in? And who says that you won't fall into the lavatory bowl one of these days, and then you won't be pulled out, or let down, as has been threatened. Then the chain will be pulled three times.

That is why you have to save it, even if it does want the whole of your hand. It is no longer disgusting at all. The finger touches the clear yellow surface, a bright ring forms around the finger tip; a ring because the yellow, the pond, the little children's pond, at first yields before the fingertip, then the fingertip draws back, but by then the yellow already has it, has placed a ring on the finger, where it half pulls itself out as one slowly pulls a peanut out of the water, whose shell was your boat. That is the yellow gleaming ring around your finger, the golden ring, a halo. For it is a sacred duty to love the bedbug. Only yesterday Anna all — as strange and as unbelievable as that perhaps sounds today — neither as an employer nor with my own hands. Well yes. As the phrase puts it so nicely, I had clean hands, although, despite my inexperience, I in fact already thought exactly as I do today about these things.

At any rate, with the death of my father I was no longer a child. I went to the post office and sent a telegram to Munich: because of an important examination it was unfortunately impossible for me to come to the funeral. That was that.

At college I gave his death as my reason for leaving. I tore up my certificate of Aryan descent, my old Hitler Youth documents, song books, membership cards and other things. Then I found out where the Refugee Committee was. There I reported my father's death as suicide for political reasons, which was believed without question. Through my transformation into an émigré my subsistence had also been taken care of, if only inadequately. I succeeded in obtaining a junior, miserably paid post with the Refugee Committee. But the work itself was child's play, the hours were short and my demands on life in those days were not yet, of course, what they are today. I lived in a dirt cheap room in a poor area; the United Nations building stands there now. The old, decayed houses were pulled down row by row to make way for its construction.

A few weeks after my transformation, when I had already learned the stupid routine work so well that I could do it without having to think, I received a letter from Miss Gröschel, my old governess, whom my father had taken on for me. I still carry it around with me even today in my wallet. There, two pictures from my childhood; on this one, behind me on the left, the small woman. As a child, of course, she seemed twice as large to me.

Miss Gröschel had spent more than ten years in our motherless house. She had brought me up from when I was three or four years old. She was clever, sometimes strict, it is true, but always fair. Exactly as one imagines a governess. She really was no tell-tale, only very occasionally did she complain to my father about me. I even believe that she did not say anything to my father when once — I must have been five or six — she had surprised me in the act of a small childhood vice. Caught me red-handed, indeed. But what I wanted to say actually concerns my father. Because I really don't believe that she said anything about it to him then. At least my father never mentioned a single word about it, and he was not the man to pass over something like that in silence. But the uncertainty, whether he knew after all and what he would say about it, tormented me for many days, and throughout that whole autumn and winter I was always ill at ease when I spoke to Miss Gröschel, or even when she simply came into the room.

That was all long forgotten of course. The letter said that Miss Gröschel had heard of my father's death and traced my address. In neat characters spread evenly across the page she expressed her sympathy at my father's demise. A model letter. When I was a child, she had also taught me to write just as beautifully. That has helped me considerably more than once in the last few years. It makes a good impression, to begin with at least, and afterwards it's already too late.

However, Miss Gröschel also had a request on her mind. She didn't come out with it on the very first page, which bore the nicely spaced out words about my departed father, but only on the next one. Miss Gröschel needed help, she needed it very urgently, for she turned to downright pleading. She had heard I was employed at the Refugee Committee, and that is why she now begged me, formally, as had always been her way, but nevertheless imploringly and full of fear, to do something to speed up her application. Everything depended on it.

She obviously overestimated my influence at the committee, for I was, at the time, little more than an errand boy, who had to order the various documents and applications which had been requested from in the archive and carry them up to the officials or carry the folders back down to the archive for the officials. But in desperation a human being tries everything possible and impossible and entertains hopes and illusions even where in reality there is little or no justification for them. Since then I have had much more opportunity to observe exactly how people behave if they are driven to despair, but even then I could already gather from her letter that Miss Gröschel was desperate.

Although one would never have noticed it and also I had never bothered my head about it, Miss Gröschel was, as she now wrote, Jewish by birth. Therefore she had to try to leave the country as quickly as possible. She knew very well just how urgent the matter was, and her thoughts with respect to this were quite correct. That could be judged very well from the vantage point of the Refugee Committee in New York. The political situation had grown more and more critical, the United States would enter the war sooner or later, and once America found itself in a state of war with Germany, then there would be no more hope of Miss Gröschel leaving the country. Conscientiously I read through her letter, with which she had enclosed two pictures from my childhood, several times, almost as though it were one of the tasks that she had given me when I was still small, always in writing, black on white, in her neat, tidy script. Then I put the letter in my jacket and went to work.

An ordinary day. In the corridors and outside the officials' offices, the petitioners, downstairs in the archive the smell of mice, tables on which forms were being filled out, documents in folders lying everywhere. Files were ordered, requested, brought up, carried in, were signed for on receipt, a bundle of documents carried up to the officials by lift, a second bundle carried down, applied for, brought up, carried in, checked off, receipt acknowledged, counted, confirmed, filed. So it went on and on and on. Not until the afternoon did I think of the letter again.

I don't even know whether it was a fine or a dull afternoon, a warm or cold day, because I had hardly glanced out of the window, and of course the committee building was centrally heated. So what nature had to say about it I don't know. In fact, nature evidently didn't have much to say about it at all. Well yes, nothing else is as real as reality, even if it sometimes becomes quite unreal. Romantics will perhaps imagine that before his first murder a young man of twenty-two will take one more good look at the world, because he will never again see it with innocent eyes. In reality, however, such a romantic way of looking at life is nothing more than a childishly sentimental vice. Such thoughts didn't even occur to me at the time.

Nevertheless it is perhaps also an exaggeration, even boastfulness, to already describe this case as a proper murder. Certainly one cannot deny my method a certain elegance, but that presumably had more to do with the unusual external circumstances, without which it would not have been possible in this form at all. Besides, it was all child's play and involved hardly any risk for me, although I did also make a few clumsy mistakes, little youthful follies, if one may call them that. Because I hadn't even clearly thought out what my intention was, at least not at the beginning. Yet, when I am alone and account to myself for everything, then even today I still call this modest performance my first murder, despite all the blunders, and it has imprinted itself on me more deeply than many subsequent events. Of course, much of what I have done, or carefully initiated in the long years that have passed since then, is much more interesting and exciting, and yet today I have already almost forgotten much of it. But how everything was then, that I still know very well.

So that afternoon I pulled Miss Gröschel's letter out of my jacket pocket, looked again at the childhood pictures that were with the letter, especially the one which also showed Miss Gröschel, and then put the pictures in my wallet. I copied the file number of Miss Gröschel's immigration request, which she had carefully printed in the top right-hand corner of the letter and underlined with a ruler. Then I ordered her file in the archive, just as I had ordered thousands of other files. When I received it, I didn't take the lift up to the offices, but used the back stairs, where there was a lavatory between floors. I locked myself in, sat down, began to smoke a cigarette and then opened the file to read it in peace and quiet. First, three passport photographs of Miss Gröschel fell into my hand. It was not without emotion that I looked at the ageing face. It still looked intelligent and was well defined, but the skin was already very wrinkled. The signature too was already a little shaky. Crow's feet, Miss Gröschel had called the first letters in my unsteady child's hand. Now she herself was writing crow's feet and also had crow's feet scribbled in the corners of her eyes and around her strict mouth.

The Gröschel case itself was quite simple and presented no difficulties of any kind. According to the official's comments it was very close to a routine favourable conclusion. There was no need at all to intervene.

I had already been forced to smile when I remembered Miss Gröschel's phrase "crow's feet". Now the smile came again. I felt it inside my face, warm, comforting, but also with a very slight touch of embarrassment. The thought of meeting Miss Gröschel somewhere in New York, on the street or down in the shabby, rattling subway, was a little funny. I saw Miss Gröschel hesitate on the edge of Central Park in the late afternoon and look at the clock, to see whether she could still risk crossing the park without being surprised by darkness and its dangers. Or I saw her in Times Square, as she walked along with a somewhat dogged expression, firmly determined not to take the least notice of the scenes around her. I felt myself taken back to earlier days, when Miss Gröschel had come to fetch me from school. I had always been a little disconcerted at the sight of her, and had usually even flinched.

I closed my eyes and came home from school. The lavatory had turned into my old nursery. Miss Gröschel's steps, which I never heard in time on the way home from school, and which had also sometimes surprised me in the nursery, were coming up the stairs.

It was not only in my memory that I heard the steps. Nothing is as real as reality. Outside, someone who must have the same walk as Miss Gröschel really was coming up the back stairs of the committee building. He passed close by my bolted door, behind which, holding my breath, I silently told myself that it was impossible for her to be in New York already.

The footsteps had unsettled me. Suddenly I was serious and quite bad tempered. Also, I had already spent too much time in the toilet, it might be noticed. I stubbed out the cigarette on one of Miss Gröschel's passport photographs and carefully put it back in the packet. Then I tore Miss Gröschel's passport

photographs, her letters, her request and her whole file into little
pieces, which I disposed of down the lavatory. I stuffed an old
newspaper, which was hanging from a nail on the wall, into the
folder. A few minutes later I handed the file over with a pile of
others down in the archive.

I was very nervous for the next three or four hours. I was not
calm again until evening, after I had written Miss Gröschel a
long, friendly letter, her documents were well on the way,
indeed, were as good as dealt with, she could put her mind at ease
and only needed to be patient for a little while longer.

Six or seven weeks later the United States entered the war. I
had not expected it so quickly at all, but of course I hadn't
counted on Pearl Harbour. Now I was sure. I knew that Miss
Gröschel would perish in Germany. Nevertheless, I was only
granted certainty by news of her death, which I received shortly
after the end of the war. It was, of course, far from true that it is
war which shows that people can be destroyed. No, war only
displays the destructibility, in itself a fundamental quality of
human beings, in an especially clear light. This clarity is perhaps
brutal, but at the same time also liberating. From this perspective
war is, after all, rather more than a youthful vice, which a still
unfree humanity cannot escape. Well.

Not that I simply advocate all that today just because I've
done it. I know that fault can be found with my procedure. For
example, I should never have given my own signature for the file
which I took out of the archive: for such an eventuality one
practises the signature of a colleague. The fact that my plan had
not even been formed when I ordered the file, does not excuse
me. It does not do to work with plans which are only half finished
and not yet thoroughly worked out, otherwise there isn't any
clean work afterwards, only sticky fingers and stained hands. It
isn't so easy to wash away; people notice it.

Tearing up and flushing away the documents was also wrong,
especially since I had a cigarette lighter in my pocket. In fact, I
should have handed back the folder with all the documents
intact and requested it again later. In the meantime I should
have taken every necessary precaution to avoid any suspicion, or

if suspicion should have arisen after all, to deflect it onto someone else, onto one of my colleagues or onto a cleaning woman. As long as it's possible to get hold of a plausible cover, one can't afford to be choosy. Well, a completely impulsive act. Let's just forget it!

At any rate, at the time I had more luck than sense. Besides, I punished myself excessively for my carelessness, because I was afraid for a long time afterwards that the business could come to light one day. I did not yet really know how little a single human being matters to an aid committee. In reality it cannot be expressed in terms of quantity at all. And absolutely nothing is as real as reality. That was demonstrated in this case too. The file was never requested again, not once. Later, at an opportune moment, I looked up the card register. No, not a thing, over and done with. The file is probably still lying somewhere today, neatly stored, unopened, with the old newspaper inside.

As I said, that was my first murder. No one is a born master, and now, of course, I have more experience and don't rely on good luck, but on the accuracy of my calculations. Nevertheless, I don't consider it good luck that Miss Gröschel really was sent to her death. I was quite right to rely on that, and I would still also defend it today. After all, the authorities over there were unusually reliable as executive organs, and with skilful exploitation of the particular circumstances, and the executive organs that they made available, as it were, perhaps no more ambitious activities could be developed at all. Experience in times like ours has also taught me, that executive organs are especially reliable precisely when they themselves don't even know whose interests they are serving. And in any case, there is never any lack of people who are ready to undertake the actual work of slaughter. In this regard one can depend on reality.

But the funny thing is that in all the years since then, during which this really was far from the only case, virtually every time right up to the present day, I still dreamed about Miss Gröschel afterwards. But she never looks as she did in the end on the passport pictures which I tore up when I substituted the old newspaper for her life. No, she is constantly changing. At first she grew thinner and thinner, until she was nothing but skin and bone, hardly big enough any more for the yellow star, which in the dreams of those days I always saw on her, on her blouse or on her coat, although in reality I don't even know whether this yellow star was worn on the blouse as well. It was far from pleasant, but on waking I shrugged my shoulders and said to myself that what happens to people, whom one has known since childhood, really does affect one. Apart from which it could not go on much longer anyway, since she was growing thinner from dream to dream. I assumed that one night she must die, or perhaps even one day, between two dreams, so that in my next dream or the one after I would probably not be bothered any more.

But that was a mistake. When she was really nothing more than a skeleton and I quite firmly assumed that she could not survive until the next dream, she suddenly became young again. She looked as she had done on the childhood picture from the time when I was five or six years old. Well. But since then she has been growing younger from dream to dream. So I'm beginning to worry about it. Because if I don't change my life, but still dream about her so vividly each time, and if she continues to grow ever younger, then it may happen, that in the end I may even have to look after her like a small child.

The Running Jump

My friend took this running jump, not I. Although I'm left standing pretty much alone today, and everyone has gone their different ways, it is simply not the case that I never had a real friend. On the contrary, I originally had so many friends that it's not true. Anyway, one of them was called John or Jones or Jonah. The name doesn't matter any more, because most of my friends are dead or have gone away or are crazy or married, but in those days he was still quite all right. Not big at all; slim, with wrists like a girl's. But he had a large head, and he was quick-tempered. Hardly had he seen the least injustice or someone looked at him the wrong way, than he turned quite pale with anger, clenched his fists — and began to run. Once he even threw away his briefcase, because it hampered him while he ran, and Max, who then took . . . But that doesn't fit in here, I only wanted to say that John — or Jonah — ran off, immediately, at full speed, up and away.

Of course people thought he was a coward. I didn't know where I was at with him either. It was not easy getting him to talk. Even after my first words he turned round and wanted to take to his heels, but I grabbed him by the collar: "Stop! Now, please, just explain to me, why . . .!?"

I confess, I too had thought him a coward, despite my friendship with him. By the way, later on he is supposed to have maintained that my friendship had only been based on my assumption that he was a coward, because it was so easy, tempting even, to be the friend of a coward. Well, we'll leave that aside. I don't believe it, of course, but after all, there really are the strangest reasons for friendships. Besides, that isn't relevant here either.

But I really had done my friend Jahn — perhaps he even wrote his name Ian or Jann, I can't remember any more — an injustice, because nothing was further from his mind than running away.

If someone looked at him the wrong way or if he noticed some unbearable injustice, then there was only one possible response: Get stuck in! Get stuck in immediately and help justice to achieve victory. Arguments are no use at all, he said, just for once I should take a look at the world we live in. Well, I didn't want to argue with him and did take a look at it. It's true: arguments are no use at all.

I think I already said earlier that my friend Johnny was not big, in fact he was rather small and not that well built either, but downright thin, slim. So if he wanted to get stuck in effectively, he had to make up for the disadvantage. That's why he took a running jump. Momentum is $\frac{m}{2}v^2$, mass over two multiplied by velocity squared. That's how he explained it to me, and it must be true, because it occurred to me that I had learned it at school. That's why I now believed the rest of what Janosch said, quite apart from the fact that he was after all my friend.

The rest was simple. Already as a small boy he had noticed that even a deserved box on the ears, smack in the gob, slap in the face, or whatever it was called there, because I really don't know any more which part of the country Juan spent his youth in — the times we live in are really far too troubled to remember that sort of thing — that such a smack in the face turned out to be considerably more effective if he had first of all taken the time and effort to draw his arm back properly. That was not always easy, for perhaps the other boy did not stand still. At the time Janusch only raised his hand against boys, never against girls.

Later he had to fight not only against school fellows but sometimes against opponents who were far superior, indeed even against adversaries who outnumbered him. One cannot always choose the circumstances in which one becomes witness to an injustice or catches a hostile glance.

So after several disagreeable experiences, he discovered that an opponent could only be overcome by a blow of superior force. But, as has been said, that force could best be attained by an extended run. Jöns had learned long before to put not only his arm, whose modest length would have set all too narrow limits on the strength of the blow, but his whole body at the service of his bellicose actions. So he ran off, in order eventually to face about and drive at full speed, an unstoppable battering ram, in among his astonished opponents, who were still laughing at his presumed retreat.

The pretence of running away also served him as a useful ruse of war. Whereas an arm drawn back to deliver a blow is virtually a spur to lightning fast counter measures, the apparent flight of the opponent lulls the one left behind into a sense of security. Up to that point everything would have been all right.

The misfortune is only that the injustices or unfriendly glances, which spurred my friend Jens on to revenge, did not usually occur in a remote, ideal landscape, but in the big city, which, after all, is the scene of almost every really decisive event in our civilisation. But for good or bad, this had as a consequence that my poor friend was virtually always impeded by adverse external circumstances in his avenging run, or running jump. Once he had to come to a halt because of the traffic lights, another time he knocked an old woman over as he was running and then had to lift her up and comfort her. Jörn after all is not made of stone, otherwise I would never ever have regarded him as my friend; yes, on such occasions he even had to wait until the ambulance had fetched her and the policeman had taken down his particulars. Bad luck, certainly, on top of all that to be pushed and threatened by the ignorant mob, which so enjoys meddling in minor accidents in the street, but that's how it is sometimes. Only very rarely are we allowed to dedicate ourselves entirely to a task without any distraction. In Jean's case, just two or three passers-by looking at a girl were sometimes enough to block the pavement and force him to a standstill, so close to the goal of his running jump that he could already see the targets of his punitive action with the naked eye. In such cases, of course, he had to run away a second time, sometimes even for a third or fourth time, in order to be able to take yet another running jump. Had he been lucky enough to avoid all the traffic obstacles, it happened that at the edge of a small park he stepped on a worm and slipped, or at the last moment tried to avoid some unfortunate, half squashed insect and so in a flash got out of his stride.

No wonder, that finally, when Jannis had overcome all these difficulties and came storming up to the place of judgement, out of breath and with hair flying, but completely full of glorious fighting spirit, the unjust and the offenders had long since left. He then usually overshot the no longer existent target by a few more yards, sometimes smacked up against a wall or into the middle of a group of foreign students, who were looking at the city, and then clumsily bolted from the scene with an embarrassed, meaningless word of apology. But he was not a coward; no, on the contrary, he was — to use a word, that in our repeatedly ruptured civilisation itself almost requires a running jump — a hero. Because in such cases it's the intention that counts, nothing else, just the intention.

So that is the end of the story, one might think. And if it's not true, then it is nevertheless well told. And if it is not well told, then there are sufficient reasons to make it impossible to tell well. For in order to be able to do that, the story teller would need to believe in it, or at least in something. Believing, that's it; either in the story or in the story telling or in the interest of the reader or listener. Either in the readiness of the listener to take him on trust, or in the readiness of an interested and interesting female listener to be seduced; or in his own ability to really enjoy such a successful seduction and to enjoy the fruits which are offered to him; or in the task of literature in our society, or as a weapon against our society or against a society, which certainly does include us, but is not really ours at all. But what if the story teller no longer believes in any of that? Well, this may sound paradoxical, but this not-believing stands in his way like a step over which one stumbles when running, because it isn't there at all. Then of course all impetus is lost, at least any authentic impetus; then, for example, the clip clop of all the different names for the old friend, Jonah, Jens, Jan, Ian, Janusch, and whatever else he's called, it's quite neat — as an idea — but it isn't authentic after all. And as long as anyone still has a story to tell and still half way believes in this story or in himself, then he won't fall for such a trick. Even if it has occurred to him and he's perhaps noted it down, he doesn't just let it stand.

Or these seemingly skilfully inserted hints, which are supposed to make the storyteller disagreeable; the platitudes of which he never tires, or the information that perhaps he only made friends with Jenö because a coward may be a particularly convenient friend — the artificial long-windedness of the whole account, which is so obviously calculated to spoil the reader or listener's pleasure in the story and to prejudice him against the story teller — it's all basically a stale trick, the desire to arouse the audience's ill-will, which one still remembers from the classroom, except that of course then it was *sympathy*, not yet ill-will, for only a citizen of lost times strives for that.

A story teller in better times would simply have said: "I had a friend called Jonah, who unjustly gained the reputation of a coward. For if someone looked at him maliciously for no reason or if he was witness to an injustice, then he drew back in order to take a running jump and strike the malicious and the wrong-doers like a bolt of lightning. But because the big city traffic with its throng of vehicles and people did not permit of freely taking a running jump, he almost always came too late, and the unjust, whom he wished to punish, had already scattered to the four winds."

That's how it would have been portrayed once upon a time. But today there's probably not a single person left, who would still have the peace of mind to catch his breath for the sake of such a story, to stand back a little, to take a running jump as it were, and then to commit the brief tale to paper so purposefully, that it strikes its target irresistibly and at the right moment. The task as such should not be despised, for the injustices and malicious glances, which even the weakest, clumsiest person would have to seek to punish, are in reality so numerous and so wicked, that even the smallest fraction of them bursts the limits of this portrayal and reveals the naked fear behind the transparent jokes and carefully laid out labyrinths.

*

But even if there was someone, like that by now far from true friend Janus or Johannes, who was unworldly or headstrong enough to take this long impossible running jump, and who, finally, like a new Jonah, would only be set down once more or thrown up closer to his predestined goal by each threatening shipwreck, by each foaming wave, by each sea monster that swallowed him up; and even assuming he got into the swing of things, which allowed him to include in his fable the ruptured life of all the overcrowded and dehumanised streets of a city which had been delivered up for judgement, and still not change course; and assuming further he now also had the possibility of publishing such an unfashionable tale, black on white, and would still not have been thrown off the track — could he then still hope that those of whom he is thinking have waited all this time and will now read his words?

No, driven on by their bad conscience or by the boredom of their own indifference, they are long ago up and away to all four corners of the compass, and the street is empty but for the thin rainbow of oil on the wet road surface, stray pieces of crumpled paper and here and there a dying insect. Perhaps the empty spot is bounded by a wall, or perhaps a group of foreign students is passing by. It doesn't matter any more, the running jump, which in retrospect appears as long as a whole life, has been wasted. Janus stands there alone. His word which has reached its target, which looks to the past and to the future, cannot reveal itself to anyone, and although apparent retreat and the absurdity of incidents encountered along the way could not rob it of any of its validity, it is suddenly no longer true at all.

Hounded to Death

At the risk of being misunderstood, I should nevertheless like to say that there can be very little, which in its way would be so grand, so stirring, not to say stimulating, and so in the true meaning of the word uplifting, as being hounded to death.

Early in the morning, when the first signal of the pursuers can already be heard, so softly and indistinctly that I, all my wits perhaps not yet about me, am unable to decide, whether it really strikes my ear from far away or from some place deep inside me — no, not strikes, rather scratches or actually buzzes, scrapes, gnaws — at the moment of awakening I am already all there. At one stroke, alert and full of vigour, I am in full possession of my physical and mental powers. Inasmuch as I can still even remember the time when I was not being hounded, it was precisely in this phase of awakening that I aimlessly frittered time away with unsightly yawns and an unworthy struggle against my own sluggishness and could often only free myself from blankets and pillows after a good half hour.

But yet this is only a single, arbitrarily chosen, unimportant example. Even a handful of examples of this kind could not remotely begin to do justice to being hounded to death — which after all is not simply a pleasure — or still less bear sufficient witness to its incomparable worth.

However, I also do not know whether the pursuers, who after all have dedicated their lives to the pursuit, to the hounding itself, would place great value on such testimonies. It is true they are always very much concerned with those testimonials and documents which, like the warrant cards of policemen on duty, verify their legal right to hunt others down. Without such confirmation and attestation they would after all never be certain of being able to shut the mouths of those who make trouble for them with all kinds of calumnies and insinuations and who try to rob them of that honour, without which even the most successful hounding to death could turn from a great task into a degrading, duty that is performed only with reluctance. No, questionable is only whether the hounders would place any importance on the verification of the *moral* justification of their conduct. The discussion of such questions appears a waste of time to them, because it threatens to keep them from their principal task, of hounding, and consequently they have devised speedier methods of dealing with moral objections and doubts of this kind. But as far as the *legal* protection of their task is concerned, they regard it as indispensable. They deploy all their powers, all the resources of their extensive transport and communications system, to protect themselves against any plan of reform whatsoever, almost to the same degree as they do to fulfil their task itself in such a way that it really deserves the name hounding, irrespective of whether their fellow creatures, whose numbers occasionally decrease somewhat if they stand in the way, understand and approve of them or not.

But I would prefer, rather, to report on what I know from my own experience and by the end of the hounding will probably know ever better, ever more precisely and vividly.

For example, apart from the heightened vigour, which I owe to my rapid awakening, there must be be mentioned the great liberation from all boredom which, as I wait for my pursuers' next signal, I now never feel in anything I undertake. The questions as to one's own duties in life also seem to be answered all at once, for being hounded itself prescribes action and inaction, efforts and goals. It does so to an extent which in earlier times was made possible only by the most encompassing, most profoundly-felt philosophy of life or perhaps by a religion which, through the painstaking search for illumination, had become personal experience.

It should also not be forgotten, that long before his fate is fulfilled, the one who is being hounded to death receives a kind of recognition through his situation, a halo which puts the artificial glorioles of all the tragic heroes of stage, film and television in the shade. Since we already know from the lives of such players how irresistible the resonance of mere roles makes the actor to many particularly sensitive women and girls, then we can easily imagine the standing that the person who is genuinely being hounded is able to attain thanks to his situation. This standing, furthermore, is so constituted that the condition to which he owes it simultaneously frees him from the many difficulties which otherwise, in a jumble of practical considerations, disappointed hopes, or fear of disappointing hopes, so often darken the lustre of the sudden emergence of human relationships before it has even had time to display itself.

Certainly, even in moments of happiness I never cease to be hounded. A car stopping in front of the house, a click on the telephone, a still indefinable noise out on the street, it can all startle me, even make me lose my composure for a moment. But on the other hand, it also helps me to experience everything with keener faculties than perhaps would otherwise be possible, and saves me from that indolence, which, even if perhaps pleasant in itself — it is already too long ago for me to be able to remember such a condition clearly — nevertheless sets an untimely end to many of the very happiest hours, minutes or moments in life and, by lulling us, turns everything pleasantly hazy and impairs consciousness and memory.

True, the question is often put to me by well-meaning people who give me refuge, during the short period of time in which we must remain inactive in some hiding place, waiting to discover whether the pursuers, whom we believe we can hear outside, have yet again not picked up the trail and so will withdraw, how I can bear never really being able to catch my breath, and whether the exhaustion which overcomes me from time to time is not so distressing, that it is perhaps not worthwhile eluding the pursuers again and again. Have I not asked myself questions like that more than once?

But such questions, comprehensible as they are, do miss the actual crux of the matter. As far as catching one's breath is concerned, just take a look at the people who have organised their lives in such a way that they catch breath frequently, even regularly. Whose breath do they catch then? Their own, or that of their wives and children and those friends, with whom one supposedly has to associate so as not to be lonely (nothing but rules for leisure which long ago made free time very unfree and even turned it into a very special kind of drudgery)? And even if they should catch their own breath, what do they do with it? What do the few people who still have breath, do with their breath?

On the other hand, as far as exhaustion is concerned, then no one can appreciate a short rest as fully as the hunted man. At the moment in which he sinks down, completely exhausted, he feels how his exhaustion, in a curious way, frees him from all responsibility, even if they catch him now, in this hour or the next, and kill or torture him. At this moment he is his only on-looker. Because he *cannot* go any further, because he *must* have some rest, he also finds it. The fingers of the one who has sunk down onto some bed or other have made themselves independent of the hounding down and, while he's still panting, they explore the roughness or smoothness of the bed cover, the line of a seam across the blanket on which he is lying, whether this seam, with its countless stitches, uniformly long or short, feels raised or sunken under his fingers, is mountain crest or ravine. Also, just at the moment of collapse, the pictures which I call to mind or which emerge of their own accord, succeed one another far more quickly and brightly than in most other situations, so that more than once the few minutes in which I had silently lain in some closet gasping for air were in reality packed so full of dramatic memories, visions and brightly coloured fantasies, that going to see a good film or a stage play could only ever be a quite inadequate substitute for what I see and hear in such moments of complete exhaustion.

It is also true, that many of those who are hounded to death do after all know — and at moments of greatest danger even feel precisely — that they are not simply suffering, but have taken, are taking, their fate upon themselves, for they are only being hounded because they have accomplished what only a few managed previously, that is, to show their pursuers for what they are. This knowledge perhaps compensates for a great deal: no longer simply to be a victim, but to have made oneself into a sacrifice, by sacrificing oneself *for* something — it can also be the struggle *against* something — or having been ready to sacrifice oneself, that is, offer oneself as a sacrifice.

No novel, no film can offer as much excitement as the life of the one who is being pursued, hounded, hounded to death. Besides, being hounded to death keeps him as fresh and young as, on the other hand, it exhausts him. It protects him from all false habits, indolence and complacency. It keeps him nimble and slim. Whenever the praises of living dangerously are sung, then one should not forget to weave into the song just a few short verses, to make being hounded down just a little more comprehensible to those born later.

Certainly, being hounded is not only a chase, an experience of heightened rhythm and feeling for life. (In this connection it is no coincidence that the word chase* popularly means great sport, amusement, exciting show, deriving from the publicly organised chasing or hunting down of animals, in which animals of the *same* species were also often set upon one another.) Like the chase put on for popular amusement, being hounded to death also of course ends in death. But even if I abhor the pathos of the old war song:

> No finer death in all the world
> Than by the foe laid low,

Then such a death is almost never as horribly senseless as a lingering death in the geriatric ward of a hospital, no death of the body that laboriously hobbles behind the death of the spirit, no slow death, but more like a death on the road, even if not on the *open* road, rather forced into a corner, bleeding on the cobble stones, beaten to the ground, half conscious perhaps, held tightly by two, three persons, while a fourth — in self defence — draws a

---

* In German 'Hetze' carries both the meaning of hounding and chase. [Trans.]

gun, points it at the head and, smiling or perhaps with a disinterested expression, carefully takes aim.

Perhaps nothing demonstrates the grandeur of being hounded to death so well as the conduct of the pursuers on and after the death of the person they have hunted down. It is almost as if they, who have hounded him for so long and finally achieved their success, were filled with envy of their victim, as if they, impressed against their will by the fulfilment of the fate, to which they have helped the hounded person, wanted to change places with him. At any rate, the myth-making as good as always begins immediately.

The interesting thing about these myths which, by the way, they give out as the pure truth, is that to some degree they try to put themselves in the position of the person they have hounded to death. The individual members of a band, who together have hounded one or several to death, willingly provide testimony for each other and declare under oath that in reality it was they who were hounded and threatened by the one who was being hounded. Their own actions, including the killing with which they finally concluded the pursuit were only to be explained, because the killed person had unrelentingly persecuted them, mercilessly pursued them, indeed driven them into a corner or possibly surrounded them. If one considers that in reality the one hounded to death — alone, or accompanied by just one or two friends, unarmed or provided with only the poorest weapons, was brought down by a whole army of pursuers, who had the most modern weapons — means of transport and communication available, to say nothing at all of financial resources, then one realises how greatly, regardless of their hostility, the pursuers, who had been at the heels of the one hounded to death, must have admired, even envied their victim. Even in death they ascribe to him the characteristics of a hero, who single-handed was able to hold at bay a force many times greater and armed to the teeth. A thousand hands, a hundred thinking heads, like an ancient Indian god, are ascribed to him. Those who killed him have always acted only in self-defence, as did their whole state and all the institutions whose servants they are. It was not an army but a self-defence force. Decisions as to the armaments of the hounders were discussed not in a ministry of war but in a ministry of defence. The assault was not directed by an assault but by a defence staff.

This also demonstrates that the pursuers, the hounders, who hound their victim to death, nevertheless also confer the final honoour on him in abundant measure, certainly by destroying him, but simultaneously by weaving a heroic legend around him, the durability of which they ensure through countless testimonies sworn on oath. The hounders therefore, whether mere pursuers or specially trained marksmen and killers, are a professional group who constantly risk their lives to increase the honour of their enemies, by raising them, if not to the heavens, then nevertheless among the romantic heroes of our age. It would not only be petty, it would be utter mockery, not to acknowledge this effort by the pursuers on behalf of the fame of those pursued by them. For one would thereby rob them of the honour, which they, often even more than others, require in order to successfully perform their sometimes very difficult profession.

Insofar as statements by the hounded themselves exist, they unfortunately often bear the traces of the headlong pace of the hunt and of the carelessness enforced by it, since such statements were often only composed in the short intervals between two stages of the hounding. The hounded person only rarely accuses his pursuers of a lack of skill and mastery of their technical equipment. But, long before he finally becomes their victim, he often falls victim to the delicacy of his pursuers, who do not wish to make his resistance to them even more difficult by allowing him, in his own lifetime, to suspect the pains they will take after his death to spread his quite legendary heroic fame. No, doubtless in order not to handicap his flight still further through ambivalent feelings towards them, they dissemble and employ all their self control. All their pronouncements sound entirely as if they consider him to be a coward, a worthless or inferior being. The more uncritically he believes in this attitude, the easier it will be for him to concentrate all his strength on the flight from them or the fight against them. Evidently they want to give him this chance. Presumably it is solely for this purpose that they lose no opportunity of insulting him with the harshest and most unjust words as soon as they come within earshot, or of beating him bloody or shooting at him, as he makes off through them with great leaps, escaping for the penultimate or even very last time. That is why those who are hounded, despite every acknowledgement of their pursuers' military discipline and determined preparedness, have no imaginative transfigurations and embellishments available, such as the hounders, in the shape of modern bogeyman and outlaw legends, have for most of their victims. There shall be no further mention here of the fact that the hounders, if they had not learned, out of a sense of tact, to hide their true estimation of those hounded by them behind derogatory and often common sounding remarks and gestures, would also be treated and described more respectfully by the hounded. It is therefore precisely this lack of selfishness and the sense of tact on the part of the hounders, which sometimes denies them the tribute, which they, better than anyone else, know is richly due to them.

And yet it is precisely here that a real understanding between hounders and hounded could lead to that greatest ennoblement of the chase, such as can never, unfortunately, be realised in the hunting of animals, because of the absence of possibilities of communication. Of course, hunters and foresters are no less convinced of the truly great worth of their activity than are the servants of a modern commonwealth, charged with the hounding by the collectivity of the people, as organised in the state, which in the execution of such duties protects freedom and democr. . .

I have lost myself in general reflections. Too late: They're coming . . . Fear . . .

The Only Difficult Thing

I know of course that I must not magnify the present difficulties between my friend and myself even further by, for example, taking offence at what he, after all, only says or does because of these difficulties. It is true that precisely during these difficult days his expressions and deeds are particularly clearly marked, if I may put it like that. Each one of them would be an excellent, a simply irrefutable example of what weighed on me in some ill-defined way in the time before the appearance of the difficulties between us, without my being able to put my finger on it. It is only now, since the beginning of our difficulties, that all these reasons have become so clear to me, that to push them aside would really be almost dishonest, and no longer show any regard for my friend.

Even though I dare not mention any of these many examples to him, in order not to make our difficulties still greater, even insuperable for him, I must, at least for my own benefit, take note of the individual examples, to protect my own thoughts from later becoming blurred, which after all could not do our friendship any good either.

Fortunately I do not find it hard to take note of these reasons, because first of all they really do stick in the mind, are indeed unforgettable, and secondly because they now unmistakably and clearly confirm what I previously experienced, at most, as quiet, not yet even oppressive doubts, so that I now feel myself to be virtually relieved of a burden, if I keep even a single one of these examples in mind.

When I take note of these individual examples, I must at the same time also carefully fix in my mind that I cannot hold any of them against my friend, mention them to him, or even silently reproach him with them. Were I to do that, then our difficulties could worsen fatally. Luckily I can easily avoid that with a little self control.

The only difficult thing for me is that the number of these examples and causes, which I must take note of and resolve not to mention at any price, is already so great and they are in themselves so tempting to use as reasonable arguments against my friend, that day after day, yes even at night, I have to recite to myself the ever lengthening lists of examples which I dare not mention to him. Because, since the beginning of our difficulties, dozens of new examples are added every day, examples with which my friend provides me in abundance, naturally without knowing it, and which I have to keep account of, as it were, in order not to make use of any of them in an ungarded moment, my whole working day and working energy is now spent in learning them off by heart, always accompanied by the thought that under no circumstances dare I mention them to my friend, not even inadvertently.

Nevertheless, a further aggravation for me is that I can never be quite sure whether I am not perhaps doing my friend an injustice through this reticence and discretion, and whether, however difficult it may be for him to look the unvarnished facts in the face, he should not, after all, have all these facts before him, so that he himself can gain a proper picture of what reproaches he exposes himself to, through his present behaviour. On the one hand, without a clear picture of that, any change and improvement is made difficult or even impossible. On the other hand, I could not help him to gain such a picture without arousing the impression of misusing every conceivable cause for reproach against him, which is of course very far from my thoughts and which could easily allow him to view the task of overcoming our difficulties in a forbidding light.

Now it is, of course, relatively easy for me not to be offended by these individual even if altogether numerous and irrefutable causes of reproach which his behaviour gives me. But since, in addition, the need to constantly plague myself with learning off by heart all these causes and exemplary cases, in order not to mention even a single one of them to him as an example, is by now such a great burden on me, sometimes I even have to resist the question whether it would not be simpler to go up to him and break his neck there and then.

Tortoise Turning

It bears nothing else as shield
Except its troubles,
Turn it, to mercy yield,
Else you too are naught but beast.
The Schilda Bestiary, Book VII. 3, 15.

Tortoises crawl across country, over damp earth, warm stones and branches, over rocky screes and through all kinds of undergrowth. When they are crawling over boulders or fallen dead wood, it can happen that they lose their balance and fall on their backs. Then most cannot right themselves again and so must die. Tortoises are tough; it takes a long time before they are dead. However, through a happy disposition, the districts in which tortoises — and consequently also their fatal accidents — are most numerous, are precisely the regions in which today the big oil companies are already spending huge sums of money to explore the potential for profitable drilling.

The oil companies, although no less armoured and to the eye of the imaginative observer no less monstrous in form than even the most singular and enormous Galapagos Tortoises, are more skilful and thoughtful in their movements and therefore, even at critical moments, always fall on their feet, never on their back. Nevertheless recently they have become increasingly troubled, because public opinion is beginning to see them as unfeeling dinosaur-like monsters, interested solely in gain. Their leading figures, weary of malicious expressions like "oil sticks", which they encounter on all sides, have for some time now been searching for conceivable ways of gaining a better reputation, if possible through not too costly, but nevertheless very conspicuous good deeds, which should, however, be without harmful effects on income or politics.

Such a possibility now presented itself to the oil companies with the creation of a new profession, for which they had to make available only an insignificant fraction of their enormous profits, a sacrifice that is more than compensated for by the resulting diminution of their unpopularity. It concerns, as the reader will probably already have guessed, the profession or the office of Tortoise Turner.

The Tortoise Turner, equipped with telescope and with electronic detection equipment, such as the American armed forces in particular had developed to track down and exterminate all surviving life in the so-called free fire zones of Vietnam, tramps or rides through or flies over, depending on the size of the subsidies provided by the oil company and the peculiarities of the landscape, the whole oil and tortoise terrain. Whenever he sees a tortoise that has fallen helplessly on its back, he turns it over, presumably also refreshes it with water and food supplies carried for this purpose, makes the appropriate entry in his log book and moves on, in order to continue his never-ending rescue work.

So, in an age in which the romantic professions are so lamentably passing away, a completely new profession has been created, which guarantees a life in the open air and harms no one, but on the contrary consists of nothing but a string of good deeds on behalf of helpless creatures.

Although the tortoise work is not directly profitable, the humane, or rather animal protective character of this activity secures for the oil companies — which finance it on a large scale — considerable sympathy, especially among the younger generation all over the world, among children, but equally among those adults who have remained young at heart, so that the operation is altogether worthwhile.

It is obvious that this profession of Tortoise Turner, founded by the oil companies, is in the highest degree environmentally friendly, not only because it makes the innocent creatures' struggle for existence less grim and dangerous. Since there is a consequent diminution in tortoise mortality, it protects the landscape of these mostly hot territories from being strewn with decaying reptile carcasses, which ultimately causes epidemics, and could certainly make the fresh air of these southern districts far less fresh.

Beyond that, however, and also beyond the benefit of which the oil companies can be certain, due to the publicising of their animal protection work and their appreciation of a romantic new profession, the creation of the professional category of Tortoise Turner has still further benefits. Behavioural studies have shown that this activity exerts a very special attraction on those adolescents who only reluctantly want to conform to our civilisation of technology and standardisation, who rebel against the bonds of urban employment, and who in general have a weakness for following their own ideas, in order — far removed from everyday profit-making activities — to improve the world.

It requires no lengthy reflection to realise that in this way, through his work as itinerant Tortoise Turner, many an enterprising young person is inhibited from becoming a revolutionary enemy within, who in the bosom of his own civilisation tends to band together with those of the same mind, to echo long refuted ideas, even to found criminal associations, and so also to become a threat, not least to those large oil companies which now, however, through their sponsorship of tortoise turning, afford him space as extensive as it is harmless, harmless simply because the rather lonely and peaceful life of the Tortoise Turner provides far more opportunity for reflection than for banding together with others, or even for conspiracies. The expanse of the southern skies above the wide savannah, through which the tortoises make their way, equally plays its part in extending the natural horizon of the young Tortoise Turner, so that beneath the stars, during nights by the camp fire or as the sun rises above the endless tortoise landscape, the petty political questions, which opponents of the big oil companies try to proclaim in their unchanging jargon under the dust and exhaust fume layer of their airless cities, suddenly appear trivial to him, even contemptible, before such a magnificent background.

So, many a young city lad, who only a few weeks before had been whistling or humming some revolutionary ditty or other, before a happy accident had made him a Tortoise Turner by way of the Voluntary Service, now fill his lungs every morning with pure, fresh air, looks up at the blue sky of the South and then sings, probably at the top of his voice, the old-new 'Turning Song', brought from his homeland and sprung from homely roots, which poetically and melodically unites concern for the environment and a sense of the true meaning of life:

> The tortoises aren't in our sight:
> They crawl and climb both day and night.
> Those who tumble will be gone!
> Each day the poor things suffer thus,
> So good soul, don't flinch or fuss:
> You must turn them, every one!
> You must turn them, every one!

Certainly it should not go unmentioned that even within the decision-making boards of the great multinational oil companies there were a few unimaginative, small minds who initially not only objected to the financing of tortoise turning, because no short-term profit resulted, but went so far as to assert that the rescue of tortoises is a sentimental, obtrusive intervention in the remorseless process of nature and, through a diminution of organic substance left to decay, could even lead in days to come to a diminution and thus scarcity in the development of *future* mineral oil reserves.

Fortunately science, impartial and objective as is its way, long ago refuted such arguments. To the best of our knowledge, tortoise matter contributed only an infinitesimally small amount to the formation of even *primeval* mineral oil reserves. But apart from that, Tortoise Turning cannot of course alter the fact that at some time or other every tortoise which makes its way across the reptile landscape must die and decay. The Tortoise Turners, on the contrary, ensure through their rescue work, that the number of these creatures grows larger than it otherwise would, because many of the successfully righted tortoises go on to reproduce again and again, before old age, some hostile animal or even, despite all the efforts of the Turners called into the field by the oil companies, a fall onto the back not seen in time leads to death. The resulting matter, which under very special circumstances could in fact become a minute proportion of the organic basis of new oil deposits, is consequently only increased by the Tortoise Turners' labour of love. Admittedly, until now not even the largest oil companies are pursuing a policy so long-term that something like organic oil field afforestation could be considered, yet for someone who believes no truth and no good deed ever quite gets lost — a belief which really must be the foundation of the tortoise work — it may nevertheless also be worth drawing attention to such a truth, no matter how apparently remote it appears to be. Quite apart from that, it has become evident that with properly coordinated company management even *oil scarcity* can be commercially quite advantageous to the oil companies.

Besides, it is hardly necessary to give particular emphasis to the fact that the number of real opponents of the tortoise work in the *upper* echelons of the oil companies is fortunately very small, otherwise the financing of the new profession and the ambitious advertising campaign for it could never have been carried through.

However, the moral significance of Tortoise Turning is also far greater than the rescue of countless harmless animals. It lies in the fact that, at the moment in which the poor creature, perhaps already in complete despair, is awaiting its death, a god-like aid, quite astonishing in its very humanity, bends down and sets it upright again, an aid whose meaning can, of course, never become clear to the tortoises themselves. Anyone, however, who has provided such aid even once in his life and has turned the fate of a tortoise at the same time as its body, falls consequently to thinking about the workings of fate and becomes in his turn aware of incomparably larger questions of existence, even if for the present these must remain just as incomprehensible, just as dark and impenetrable as is the activity of the Tortoise Turner to the tortoise set upright by him. The horizons, however, which such thinking opens up are wider than the usual instrumental thinking of our age, to the same degree that the great endless southern tortoise landscape is wider than the cramped cities in which that instrumental thinking was at home.

That human beings, and not only the oil companies, but also the Tortoise Turners, thereby help themselves by fulfilling a commandment of universal altruism with regard to these humble animal victims, is only further cause to render account to ourselves, how, in a world which at times appears to have increasingly little meaning, again and again like the stars in the night sky, individual points of light whose beneficial significance must remain beyond all doubt, burst into flame. As long as new vocations such as that of the Tortoise Turner can emerge, then the life of human beings on earth can also not be quite without meaning and purpose.

My Doll in Auschwitz

I came to Auschwitz as a visitor in April 1967, two days after a big memorial service. The signs on all the roads, which indicated the way to the old extermination camp, were still new and shiny. The stones at the memorial to the murdered were also visibly freshly hewn, but the wreaths were beginning to fade, and the rain and the ash-laden dust had already left their mark on the black ribbons.

I had been afraid. On the journey through the Polish countryside with its brightly coloured and ornamented wooden houses reminiscent of Chagall, I had secretly hoped for a breakdown, for a minor accident just serious enough to prevent us reaching our destination. But no accident held us up. The weather became ever brighter, the farmhouses recently washed clean by the light rain became ever friendlier in the sun, which emerged between the clouds more and more often. The farmers were not doing badly, and the houses were well looked after. Some were painted blue or had blue carved corner beams. A Polish friend, who was travelling with us, explained the display of colour to me: houses or beams were painted blue, wherever a marriageable girl was living.

Another village, another one, yet again one with a beautiful old wooden well. The road signs with their torch (which signified the camp or the burning of the dead or the fire of remembrance, burning grief) did not let us go. Finally we were past the last village and stopped in front of the entrance to the camp.

Kiosks, picture postcards, refreshments, tourists. Also a group of soldiers who had just been dragged through the camp. Above the old camp entrance in cast iron letters "Arbeit macht frei" — "Work Makes Free." The lamps at the entrances to the houses of the old principal camp also had cast iron ornamentation. A taste for craftsmanship. German craftsmanship. Everything exactly as described by Peter Weiss in his report *Meine Ortschaft* — 'My Place'. I had read the description of his visit to Auschwitz once more during the night, in order to prepare myself for what I had to see.

The preparation made it a little easier. Being able to hold on to what could be recognised again, to what I had already read, which had been described and recorded black on white was a help against anxiety and against the shivering — although the sun was shining, it was a cold morning. Being informed is always simultaneously the beginning of getting used to something. A feeling perhaps faintly reminiscent of the satisfaction with which tourists equipped with a Baedeker identify the characteristic features of a landscape or a city after a glance at their book.

No, not satisfaction, but nevertheless diminution of the horror, at least that short-term diminution through remembrance of what has been read, through recognition of what one already has in one's head anyway. So here too the completely unbearable became for a few seconds almost bearable. For example, the mountain of hair, cut from the gas chamber corpses, before they disappeared into the furnaces built by the company of Topf & Sons, was there, simply there, in the right place, as the law had decreed it, as I had read it. There to be attested to, but to my relief already attested to by Peter Weiss. Also from photos that I had seen. It was higher certainly, this mountain of hair, and it was not simply a great mound, as I had expected, but flat. The hair looked different too, much more varied than I would have thought possible, and unexpectedly lustreless. Under glass now, but it had not always been. In fact it only shone like beautiful girls' hair in the upholstery cloth, into which the hair of the dead had been worked up, which was displayed nearby. I had also already read about the cloth and the cushions stuffed with human hair. Now I could confirm that it is true. On the spot. Something was still in order there, horror in its place, almost bearable.

I had expected the mountain of shoes, I had also read about it and seen photos. Certainly it too was larger than I had imagined, and I had never actually thought about the many children's shoes. But even that was still to some extent bearable. The first real surprise was a huge heap of spectacles. I had also, it is true, not expected the pile of artificial arms and legs, but it was not so large, possibly because the Second World War had made artificial limbs into desirable, scarce goods, so that they were always quickly forwarded to users in the Reich and larger quantities could never accumulate here in Auschwitz. As I said, the pile of artificial limbs was not so large. At any rate the spectacles were more impressive.

Perhaps because they all looked old-fashioned. Understandable. After all there *could* not be models from the last two or three decades among them. Perhaps also because spectacles play with the light in a curious way, when so many are thrown into a heap. With their rusty metal frames some looked like hastily sketched spiders or scorpions. At some point these spectacles must have been in the rain or snow, because many lenses were clouded. The whole pile of spectacles looked at least as dead as the piles of corpses which I had seen in concentration camp photos after the war.

Even more surprising was the mountain of children's toys. I could not remember ever having read anything about it, not even in Peter Weiss. Or had I quickly wanted to forget it? Apart from that I had children myself, and that didn't make it any easier. But an old letter from a guard or camp employee, which hung behind glass on the wall in one of the extended stone buildings in the old principal camp, showed that his reaction to the toys had been quite different. Transferred to Auschwitz with wife and small child and obliged to make a prompt start on this tour of duty, even before he had been able to make the most urgent purchases, he now requested the camp authorities to provide him with a pram, nappies, children's clothing and toys from the stocks accumulating here, possibly on loan, Heil Hitler.

Somewhat helplessly I looked at the pile of toys partly damaged, partly well-preserved. Suddenly I saw Moritz. Moritz was about ten inches high, red haired, with a green jacket and green trousers. He was on wheels, so that when he was pulled along on the string, he alternately bent forward and leant back. At the same time he also swung his arms and legs. It wasn't me pulling him along on the string; I was separated from him by a glass barrier, but I knew exactly. It was a reunion. Moritz had been my own doll, broken when I was four years old, but now completely undamaged. As a child I had of course never considered that Moritz was mass produced. I cannot remember either ever having seen a second Moritz in a toy shop or in the park where I played. Only in Auschwitz, more than forty years after my doll was broken, did I see its double.

From this moment on Auschwitz had a new dimension for me. It was no longer just the unimaginable other, the completely alien and dead, instead something strangely familiar had emerged out of the emptiness and emerged again and again. The household goods in the principal camp, such as the camp staff had used, were not always unfamiliar. This wooden ladle, had it not been in our kitchen in Vienna, in Alserbachstrasse, long before the Nazis took over, before my father was murdered and our apartment wound up? And here, on the wall, this spice box! Earthenware, white glaze, with fancy labels: flour, semolina, sugar — and smaller drawers with the words: caraway, pepper, saffron. That was my grandmother's spice box. It was so unmistakeable, that I could only think "spice box", and even now, while writing it down, I cannot yet think of the right name, because we had only ever called the heavy thing that hung on the kitchen wall and which had once almost fallen on me, spice box, although that term could refer at most to the smaller drawers for caraway, paprika and pepper and not to the larger drawers for flour, rice, semolina and sugar. Like my mobile doll, Moritz, our spice box too had at some time or other, when my grandfather had bought it, been a mass produced object. Everything else is easy to explain, because many people, old ones from my grandmother's generation or younger ones from my parent's generation, who had already inherited the old household goods, were deported to the East, "for re-settlement," as it was called. In some cases they even had to pay travel expenses for their re-settlement as well, and full of hope they took a few of their smaller household objects with them. So had the spice box with the fancy blue writing come to Auschwitz. Not with my grandmother. She too had been gassed, it is true, at the age of seventy-six; but she had already arrived at her penultimate station, at Theresienstadt, without heavy luggage, because she was blind and frail and could not carry very much.

In Auschwitz I saw old fashioned brown shoes with a very particular kind of leather bow, such as I had not seen for many years. Only on seeing them did I remember that my nurse had worn those shoes. I saw the greatest variety of small ornamental objects that the camp personnel had appropriated to embellish their rooms and offices. Some members of our family, through whom such stuff had landed in our household, had evidently had the same bad taste as the SS.

The most lively and surprising memories are attached to details that are especially unlikely or minor. In one of the stone buildings, still in the old principal camp, I entered an almost bare room. Only empty petrol bottles piled up in one corner. Little bottles of thick moulded glass. The mould lines running from the neck to the bottom were clearly visible on the sides of each bottle. The bottles were squat necked, the transition from the body to the neck was not finely curved, but ended suddenly and abruptly in a stubby cone which, shortly before it came to a point, disappeared, equally abruptly, into the neck of the bottle. On each bottle a red adhesive label, which was not transparent but a little translucent. Printed with plain but nevertheless old fashioned letters: "Petrol — Handle With Care! Inflammable!" The petrol bottles of my childhood which for me were directly related to the death by fire of Paulinchen, who in *Struwwelpeter* had remained at home alone. I had been lectured for years about handling them carefully. I had left Vienna and Hitler's domain on 4th August 1938. Since then I had never seen these thick glass bottles with the red adhesive labels again. Also, I had never thought about them again, but now, in Auschwitz, they were old friends.

The woman who was our guide through Auschwitz had herself

been an inmate of the camp. From her we learned how the petrol bottles had collected in the bare room. Here, petrol-soaked cotton wool was introduced into various orifices of girls and women from the office and then lit. They had been detected trying to smuggle letters from one camp to another or even to the outside world. This happened again and again. So the old familiar petrol bottles of my childhood had been preserved here.

Repelled by the lively trade at the kiosks and refreshment stands in front of the camp entrance, I had from the outset decided to take no memento from Auschwitz home with me. But I did not hold to that. Even before going to the first house after I had been to the "small gas chamber", I had already picked up a stone.

Auschwitz — the old principal camp with its former barrack buildings and with the "small" gas chamber, not Birkenau with its large, demolished gas chambers — is full of pebbles. The camp inmates themselves had to fetch the stones from the nearby stream and scatter them evenly. Such quantities of ashes and bone fragments from the crematoria were thrown into the deepened stream bed in their place that even today, when the water level is low, a layer of fused bone fragments becomes visible. The pebbles are mostly primary rock, sometimes there is also a piece of brick among them, whose rough edges have been worn smooth by the water. One of the rock pebbles had caught my eye. It was oddly shaped and reminded me of the lumps of flint on the south coast of England, except that it was much smaller. One surface was quite smooth and seemed to have a drawing scratched on it, perhaps a mother who was holding a small child in her arms. I could not decide whether someone had really drawn on this stone, or whether I was just imagining it. Finally, thoughtfully, I put the stone in my pocket, where I only found it again days later.

I also found two of the other three mementos from the camp, almost simultaneously. The third, if one can describe it as *a* piece, a unit at all, was given to me. All three were from Birkenau, the big extermination camp. When I got there I had already spent hours in Auschwitz, the old principal camp, and followed, somewhat dazed, still registering impressions, but almost without any feeling and also — as I later discovered — without noticing my increasing tiredness, behind the former camp inmate who was our guide.

At one point she had left us alone for a few minutes, on the almost idyllic meadow in Birkenau, on which millions of people had to strip naked before they were led into the gas chambers, which are now almost all destroyed and more or less hidden by the trees growing at the edge of the meadow. I had an SS photo of the people on this meadow in my mind, some naked, some half naked. Here, where I was standing, they had undressed by the hundred. "If I scrape with my foot now," it occurred to me, "then I'll find a button." I scraped very lightly with the tip of my shoe, wet and gleaming from the grass. There lay the button, small, whitish in front of my black shoe, much lighter than the grey-brown earth. A little mother-of-pearl button, from a shirt or a piece of underwear, already somewhat weathered and fissured by frost. When I bent down for it, I also found a knife in the grass, the big rusty kitchen knife. The blade had continued through the wooden handle, which must have consisted of two parts and been attached to the iron on both sides with rivets. The rivets were still there, but only remnants of the wood, and they fell apart in my hand. One could still kill a person with the knife today. But whoever had brought this knife with him to the meadow of Birkenau and presumably hidden it in the grass there, in order not to draw any attention to himself, had probably allowed himself to be led into the gas chamber without resistance. Because otherwise the knife would have been taken to the principal camp of Auschwitz by the scrupulous SS as evidence against him and not left lying in the grass in Birkenau. Button and knife I took with me, but I lost the button again, or I have forgotten where I put it.

Perhaps half an hour after the discoveries on the meadow we came away from the demolished ruins of the "big" gas chambers and turned our backs on them. When we had stopped to breathe in the fresh air and let the sun shine on us, our guide bent down, lifted some of the damp sand which was everywhere around and crunched softly under our shoes, and put a little of it in each person's hand. We should see what kind of soil we were walking on here, she explained. In the fine, pale sand we saw little grey and white bone splinters. Actually I can only say of myself that I saw them, because we did not say anything and no longer exchanged impressions, as at the beginning of our walk through the camp. I had not said a thing for some time and did not say anything now either. I had also long ago lost my fear that I would start to weep in Auschwitz. I was unaware of feeling anything more. If anything, the damp dust and sand with the bones made me even calmer than I had been before. Over a length of time, it was all almost soporific. Nothing else surprised one, not even the big round cisterns set in concrete, with their adjustable stops, which had been used to separate the fluid content of one half from that of the other. One noted that these cisterns had been filled partly with chopped-up corpses, partly with acids. There had been experiments on the chemical utilisation of corpses. It was explained to us that the process had, however, proved economically unprofitable. One heard and took note of this and everything else, but no longer allowed oneself to be upset by it. Not by anything any more.

Yet only a few hours before, in the principal camp, the discovery of a typing error had caused me to exclaim out loud. A note from the commandant at the time of the most intensive activity in the camp had said, that before entering the gas chamber, the Jews' possessions — *Habseligkeiten* — were to be taken from them under a pretext and safeguarded, Heil Hitler.

Only someone had made a mistake and typed *Halbseligkeiten* — half blessednesses — instead of *Habseligkeiten*. To err is human. Nevertheless I called out loud to the others. It occurred to me that during my childhood we referred to someone deceased as the blessed. Also a passage in Ilse Aichinger's book *The Greater Hope* — the suicide of the Jewish grandmother, who wants to avoid deportation to the extermination camp — occurred to me. "The body poor in spirit on the path from poverty to blessedness" "Der armselige Leib auf dem Weg von der Armut zur

Seligkeit", Ilse Aichinger had written of the dying woman. Half way there. Half blessedness.

I no longer know how we got out of the vast camp complex again. I saw nothing more, not even in the low barracks, about which Peter Weiss says in his description: "Here the breathing, the whispering and rustling is not yet quite hidden by the silence, these bunks . . . are not yet quite abandoned." No, everything was completely abandoned, and if anything breathed and rustled a little, it was only I. Nothing whispered, because I was alone in the hut, without the others, and without our guide, and I was dumb.

Not until some time later, on the return journey, did I notice that I was weeping, but silently. I reached into the pocket of my plastic raincoat for my handkerchief and when I pulled out my hand it was white. Lost in thought I had put the sand with the bone fragments in the pocket and the warmth of my body had dried it. What I had thought to be fine, pale sand, had been mostly ashes. At night, in the hotel, when I turned out my coat pocket, I could not easily throw away the dust and bone fragments which fell onto the newspaper spread out on my table. Down the lavatory? Into the wastepaper basket? Morosely I at last put it into a little empty pill box, which I have never got rid of since.

There is still one thing or another that could be reported. For example, about the drawings and sculptures with which former inmates tried to register life in the camp — or death in the camp. Many of these works are clumsy and in their honest laboriousness and uneasy awkwardness make the objects of the Auschwitz Museum, among which they are displayed, almost bearable. I don't know if that is so bad. If the unbearable remains unmitigatedly unbearable, then that is for most people no reason not to bear it any longer and, perhaps, change the world in such a way that there is nothing unbearable any more. It is just a reason to forget the unbearable as quickly as possible and to no longer think about it, even if much that is likewise unbearable continues to exist or is even threatening. The unbearable, however, once awareness of it has established itself in my mind, continues to have an effect long after I have recognised the clumsy work of art, the typing error or the chance memory of an old doll, which stimulated it, as a grotesque irrelevance, which has only borrowed its significance from the unbearable itself. And yet such details can make possible a leap from one's own fear and dread to insights and reflections, and even lead to over-coming fear with the help of what one was most afraid of. I shall never again have the fear of having to see Auschwitz, which I had on that day in April 1967.

What the Facts Were

An attempt is made here to subject a single brief event to a reasonably precise investigation. It would of course also be possible, for the purposes of such an experiment, to refer to an episode in Vietnam or Cambodia, in South Africa, Pakistan, North or South America. But in order to avoid any embarrassment, such as can so easily arise from current day to day politics, an incident will be reported here from a period which has long ago been incorporated into the history of the past and transfigured, as it were, by film and television, by novels and memoirs. A closer study is also made easier, since the verdict on the inhumanity of those days appears far more unanimous than it does on crimes and excesses that are still continuing or that have only recently occurred. The case is as follows.

One day a few of those who were not taken to the gas chambers right away are said to have called out at the end, "Watch out, we don't burn well! More will be left of us than you bargained for! Our smoke will suffocate you!"

These were their last words before they burned. Their predictions have not, however, come true. They burned well, very well even, care had been taken of that. Although petrol was already in short supply then, it had not been spared, and had been poured or sprayed on most shortly beforehand. "Emergency baptism" it was called by the others, who drove them into the fire, the last part with long poles, in order not to come too close to the flames themselves.

Not one of the drivers and commanders of the drivers were suffocated by the smoke of those burning. From experience they knew very well how far back they had to stand and also that they had to take account of the wind. And since these burnings, which they used to call "Minor Resettlement Without Special Facilities", were basically an insignificant, little noticed episode, which was not to be compared to the simultaneous so-called "Major Resettlement Action" with the Zyklon-B crystals manufactured by Degesch, the German Pest Control Company [Deutsche Gesellschaft für Schädlingsbekämpfung], they also did not attract much attention, and some of the burners who later returned to their homeland, still live today as respected elderly gentlemen in their postwar professions, or as pensioners, loved by their grandchildren. The last words of the burned were therefore mistaken at best.

To be precise, and today being precise is rightly considered just as important as objectivity and detachment, as a condition, before one can venture simply to speak of the true or even of the desirable — to be precise, one actually cannot even concede to the burned a really honest mistake, made in good faith.

One only has to stick to their own words, which belong to everyday language and are easily understood, and then analyse them impersonally, impartially, regardless of opinions and systems, entirely without prejudice, soberly and relying on healthy common sense.

So finally those who were burned called out to those who were burning them: "We don't burn well! More will be left of us than you bargained for," and in addition the words: "Our smoke will suffocate you!" Now of course one can allow those burned, who, when all is said and done, had death staring them in the face at the moment of these exclamations, intense distress, comprehensible protest against their sad fate, anger at those burning them and much more besides. All of that, however, no matter how much it may appeal to our sympathies is irrelevant to an investigation aiming to establish the facts, indeed must be left out of consideration and be swept aside, so as not to obstruct our view. Here it can only be a question of investigating whether these last words comprised factually correct statements or genuine mistakes or even conscious deviations from the facts, as they were known to the speakers.

Now one must realise, that even before it was their turn to be burned, those who called out had been forced to look on more than once as others burned, and indeed, which is important, under the same conditions as themselves, insofar as their burners, who disposed of a considerable degree of practice and skill, could ensure a uniformity of conditions. They — meaning of course those designated for burning — must therefore have known how well they too would burn under the given circumstances, which they were familiar with and which after all had not changed, and how easy it would be for the onlookers, the organisers of their burning to avoid, not, it is true, the smell, indeed perhaps not even an occasional irritation of the throat, but nevertheless, at any rate, being suffocated by their smoke.

Also, the supposition that they could meanwhile have forgotten their own previous observations as witnesses of such burnings, for example, as a result of indifference and blunting of the senses which is well known to have been extremely widespread in these camps, is at least highly improbable, especially if one considers that among those at whose incineration they had been present, were, in many cases, their own parents, spouses and children. No, they must have known all that from experience. So, with their last cries to their tormentors, they were not simply mistaken, and despite every sympathy one cannot avoid the conclusion, that they — whatever their motive may have been in doing so — consciously deviated from the facts known to them, and died with deliberate distortions, not to say lies, on their lips.

They could, however, have meant it differently. They could have intended in the end to shout out a *poetic* threat, as it were, to their burners. But as comprehensible as this motive may be to us, especially if we try to place ourselves in the truly pitiable situation of the burned, this motive nevertheless shares the fate of all agitation and propaganda which does not stick rigorously — sine studio et ira, as the Ancients said — to the facts: one understands the motive and is annoyed. Or, to stick to the facts here too, "One's conscious of the intention, and put off," for thus, and not otherwise, freed from its usual falsification, runs, word for word, the quotation from Goethe's *Tasso*, Act II, Scene 1.

But to return to our sad theme. Even with the best will in the world one, leaving all else aside, cannot spare those who called out the threats, from the accusation of not having acted consistently. For on the one hand they evidently did still want to speak to their burners, but on the other they apparently did not make the effort to offer them a key for the better understanding of their words. They would only have had to insert in their cries the words ''as it were'' or in the end have cried out: ''We mean that in a symbolic sense, understand us properly.'' Then at least they would have been able to die in the knowledge of having done everything that was in their power to make themselves understood.

Certainly one ''feels'' — let the verb used by Goethe be permitted here too — one *feels*, therefore, that it may have been their extreme suffering itself which has played such a nasty trick on their formulations. But despite every sympathy which is undoubtedly in order here, clarity must never be sacrificed to suffering. They remain two separate things.

The especially unfortunate formulation, ''More will be left of us than you bargained for,'' must in addition be ascribed to the circumstance, that the callers — many of whose educational careers had already been interrupted by years of persecution — had neither the requisite knowledge nor the time and intellectual practice, to reflect on what they were actually shouting. Even under much more favourable circumstances, how much other people have bargained for can hardly be determined. The words ''more than you bargained for'' must, therefore, among other things, have been simply a clumsy error on the part of these unfortunates, which we can therefore disregard.

Fortunately these tragic events, which are now also even more difficult to check because of their remoteness in time, are, by their nature and magnitude, so far beyond our capacity for verification, that a philosophy aiming at precision can, with good reason, refuse to concern itself with such matters at all. However, as far as our own modest investigation, which aspires only to a reasonably precise application of our everyday critical capacities, we can say in conclusion: The same is true of any episode, if one makes the effort simply to show what the facts were.

The Big Show

In May 1971 semiliquid magma rolled down Mount Etna towards the villages below, and the tourists regarded the volcanic eruption as an unforgettable holiday gift. The police could hardly hold them back any more, as the slow stream of lava destroyed first a bridge and then approached the nearest houses, from which farmers attempted, until the last moment, to rescue all their movable belongings.

The excitement of the tourists was further heightened by the apparent slowness of the molten mass of rock. More than once tourists, who could no longer bear the waiting, were heard shouting, "Faster! Faster!" or "Hurry up!" This encouragement was not for the benefit of the farmers concerned to save their possessions.

It is true that the farmers were also closely observed and occasionally snapped by the tourists, but in the eyes of the sightseers or by now sight-addicts, they were of no great interest, but comparable, for example, to the extras in a big show or perhaps to the worn-out nags in the arena where the real interest lies in the bull and the matador, and sympathy for those miserable creatures is summoned up for a moment, at most, if the bull has just slit yet another one open.

A tourist hardly ever offered to help the farmers with the salvage operations. Money yes, a mixture of tip, conscience money and compensation, that occurred often; but not help in carrying furniture, bed clothes, bird cages or images of saints, baskets or jugs. It would also have seemed incongruous to some tourists, as if they were suddenly expected to jump onstage and intervene in the action. It's not done.

When the lava reached the first house, and set the beams

alight and flattened the walls, whose plaster had begun to crumble in the heat, the tourists held back by the line of police began to clap and cheer loudly. The farmers, perhaps enraged that these tourists apparently sided with the lava rather than with them, began to throw stones and shout threats at them, so that the police found it necessary to intervene more than once. As a result fences, vines and farming implements suffered as well as people.

Later it emerged that the tourists, in surging back and forward across vineyards, fields and meadows in search of wherever the show was at its best, had caused more damage than the lava.

The Patriotic Fitting

The most remarkable monument to a great man that I have ever seen is small and is made of glazed English porcelain. It represents Napoleon and, although at the time it was mass produced in many versions, not unlike the much larger moustache busts of the Stalin era, it is today a rare and consequently expensive collectors' item. For the brightly glazed bust of Napoleon rises up exactly in the middle of a chamber pot.

It would be too superficial to regard this merely as a curiosity, as an odd plant, as it were, from which English patriotism of the Napoleonic period put forth blossoms. Here we are also confronted by a colourfast, washable product of entrepreneurial spirit, which was able to creatively unite initiative and patriotism. For the production of these patriotic multi-purpose objects basically arose less from a love of functional commercial art than from speculation on considerable profits. This was presumably fulfilled to a greater degree than in the case of the building speculator who, stimulated by a similar mixture of ingenious acquisitive spirit and concrete, if less patriotic political considerations, and convinced of Napoleon's imminent victory, built a whole square of small but elegant houses in the west of London, between Earls Court and Holland Park, for the French occupation officers and then went bankrupt because he could not dispose of the small residences intended for Napoleonic officers who never landed. It goes without saying that today these houses are almost prohibitively expensive.

But back to our chamber pot: One can imagine how healthy the sudden association of the hitherto unmentionable metabolic functions with a new patriotic activity, which was furthermore altogether pleasing to God, must have been for the physical and moral well-being of its owners. The automation of this association has produced a counterpart perhaps only in those modern Tibetan prayer wheels, which bore their OM MANI PADME HUM on the rotating parts of electric motors and so yielded a prayer for each revolution. These prayers, by the way, also aided liberation, however only from Samsara, the whole earthly vale of tears with its wheel of sorrow, and not from its organic waste products as well as from a prominent national enemy.

Now, however that may have been, the multi-purpose chamber pot made it possible for the user to satisfy his patriotic needs without any additional efforts. Suitably relieved, the more direct contest with the national enemy could then be left to others. We should also not forget that this was by and large a quite bloodless — assuming the owner's good health — method of conflict with an opponent, even if aesthetically perhaps somewhat disreputable. It is therefore possible to regard the now rare multi-purpose utensil, not unreasonably, as the modest forerunner of later — and, despite the collectors prices which have meanwhile climbed to undreamt of heights, nevertheless much more costly — organisations like the League of Nations and the United Nations, whose moral and practical effectiveness is comparable in some respects to our brightly coloured and easily manipulated utensil. At any rate, the users and enter-prising manufacturers of the old multi-purpose utensil already recognised the importance of such safety valves, which offer the possibility of giving free rein to one's feelings in a harmless manner and so of freeing oneself of things, which could otherwise accumulate inside the body and become toxic.

On further reflection another characteristic feature of the brightly coloured object also appears modern. The users may have believed they were striking at Napoleon and suitably humiliating him through use of their artistic industrial product. But in reality only their domestics suffered, because the cleaning of a vessel which was ornamented inside with a statuette was, of course, considerably more difficult than that of an ordinary chamber pot with a smooth bottom. What is familiar from our own time, is the circumstance that the domestics evidently never complained about this extra work in the service of patriotism and the common effort, at least not insofar as we can trust the historical sources. On the contrary they will have felt more closely bound to their masters through the intimacy of the utensil. This readiness to perform dirty work in the name of a real or merely imagined national or cultural community, or commonwealth, or inspiration by common goals, even where one is in reality strictly excluded from use of the objects concerned, has, even today, not yet exhausted its role in upholding state and society.

The Artificers

Nothing can better refute the assertion that the well-off in their comfortable apartments and villas are corrupted by their pleasant conditions of life and bow down to everything, than the story of the "Tool Makers" or, more accurately, the "Artificers," as they called themselves shortly after their formation, in order — already with the choice of this foreign name — to secretly oppose the Germanomania of the hated regime.

The Artificers belonged almost entirely to the liberal professions. Doctors, architects, scholars, artists and teachers, old enough still to have known Wickersdorf and the Wandervogel Youth movement, met here in the pleasant suburbs and after lengthy deliberations developed their own and highly original form of taking up the struggle against the ruling tyranny and its crimes.

Strikes, factory sabotage and so on were of course out of the question for them and few would have been suited even to distributing leaflets. Most were either too old or simply too conspicuous. There were striking figures among them, and in an emergency they would probably not have been able to run fast enough either.

Thanks to their social position they were infinitely better informed than the average person. They not only knew how to read between the lines of the newspapers, but in their villas they were out of earshot of unknown informers. Protected from snooping strangers by gardens and faithful servants, they could listen to foreign radio stations, their knowledge of other languages being of benefit to them. Also, through their professions or, if they were already retired, through their former professions, they had numerous contacts, thanks to which they learned a great deal. Concentration camps and gas chambers, medical experiments on human beings, they found out about it all, and that is what they concentrated their struggle against.

Long before the first gas chambers were even being planned, still less being built, they had already asked themselves what would be needed, to free people from the big camps. They had procured wire cutters for the barbed wire, even to some extent made them themselves, since the purchase of such tools was now, after the outbreak of war, no longer so easy and without risk. When, at their next meeting, two younger members of the circle had drawn attention to the fact that the barbed wire of the perimeter fencing was often electrified, then the real work of the Artificers had begun.

First, the handles of the pliers and wire-cutters were covered with insulating material, then protective suits against electric shocks were designed, and in the course of a few weeks actually produced, and finally two scientists who belonged to the group also invented a kind of portable lightning conductor, which they made themselves and tried out in their private laboratory. When the new apparatus had successfully withstood all tests, it was manufactured in large quantities in order to be ready in an emergency.

These portable lightning conductors were nevertheless the only construction with which the Artificers had a mishap. On the occasion of an official lumber clearance — an air raid precaution — two inspectors, who came unannounced, stumbled across a large number of the new appliances and asked suspiciously, but perhaps only in the somewhat guarded, almost furtive manner of joking, which the servants of the regime had picked up, whether that might be a secret weapon. The owner of the villa, one of the two scientists, did not quite lose his head at that, but was nevertheless somewhat disconcerted, and to get out of the situation finally found it necessary to lie to the two men in uniform, that it was indeed an important military invention, which he wished to put at the disposal of the armed forces.

It is true that the risk to him and the other Artificers was fortunately thereby removed, and the inspectors who had emptied a few glasses of schnaps to the success of the new secret weapon, departed in good humour. Only there was now really nothing else the old gentlemen could do, except put the invention at the disposal of the armed forces. The value of the appliance for attacks on enemy positions with electrified barbed wire was self-evident, the models were all collected, the inventor received a letter of thanks and about two years later, when the apparatus had conclusively proved itself in the war, even a medal and a reward.

The Artificers were so depressed at this unfortunate incident, that in the end they did not even reproduce this appliance for their own purpose of breaking through electrified concentration camp fences. They simply could not bear to be reminded about it, and let matters rest with their insulated wire-cutters.

Instead, however, in years of silent but inventive work, numerous other important and useful constructions were designed and perfected by them. The whole resistance circle — to mention only one example — understood very clearly, that in view of the desperate condition of those to be liberated and the probable resistance of the camp guards, only the best, most effective instruments would be good enough for the liberation of the unfortunates and for the subsequent first aid. Consequently the villas of the Artificers became, in the course of time, veritable arsenals of tools, drugs and cleverly contrived appliances, if arsenal is the proper word for these objects dedicated exclusively to peaceful and humanitarian purposes, beginning with the sheets of metal with which the tyres of the rescue vehicles were to be protected from damage on their way across the broken barbed wire of the camp fences to the first-aid packets, with glucose and milk chocolate, and the antiseptic water filters for combatting typhus and other infectious diseases. Even sleeping gas pistols for the harmless neutralisation of incorrigible members of the camp guard were not missing. The Artificers had foreseen that such stooges of the tyrannical regime would perhaps try to prevent their rescue work. In order not to endanger the pacific character of their picture of the future, they had either overlooked or did not want to admit that liberated camp inmates could hinder their jailers in their further activities even without sleeping gas pistols.

Later, when they learned of the construction of the first gas chambers, the stock of rescue appliances increased in proportion to the new sad necessities. Breathing apparatus, atomisers to spray chemicals which could render the Zyklon-B gas harmless, and peculiar gadgets which looked a little like vacuum cleaners, but were air replacement appliances for gas chambers opened at the very last moment. There was even a kind of stretcher with oxygen mask for the rapid evacuation of dangerously ill camp inmates, which could be attached to a helicopter by strong suspension gear, to convey the patients to the nearest large hospital without any loss of time. For it goes without saying that the actual application of this rescue apparatus, just as of the other constructions depended on the possibility of organising land or air transport as well as adequate police and escort units.

With that too the Artificers concerned themselves heart and soul. But since this part of the rescue plans did not belong to their actual area of operation and since they could only undertake attempts to initiate the necessary contacts with the greatest care and secrecy because of the terrorist and violent character of the ruling system, to which of course their efforts were entirely opposed, they only succeeded now and then in finding a potentially useful ally in the preparation of this part of their plans. Even then the progress of their efforts usually faltered after a short time. Once the newly found ally disappeared without trace, perhaps himself arrested and sent to one of the camps, on another occasion these contacts could, after lengthy efforts, only report insuperable difficulties. So week after week and month after month passed.

During this difficult time of increasing air attacks on the capital — in whose pleasant suburbs they had stored their supplies, so that a part of their rescue apparatus lying ready for use was also occasionally destroyed and had to be replaced — they could easily have lost hope. On the one hand, however, the unceasing work of securing and constantly replenishing their rescue appliances helped them over hours of discouragement, on the other hand, they always took heart again, when they met, by describing to each other how children saved from the gas chambers at the last moment would throw themselves, laughing and weeping, into their arms, and how the mothers and fathers in the camps would tear open the first-aid packages with chocolate and glucose and bless them, the Artificers, for their dangerous and wearisome, but ultimately all the more successful secret struggle for the tools and means of mass rescue. This thought always lent them new strength.

It is true that today we know that, in the end, the deployment of the rescue aids for which the Artificers had striven so earnestly and tirelessly, failed to take place; yet nothing would be more mistaken, even petty, than simply to dismiss, therefore, their efforts as futile.

No good influence is ever completely lost. One only has to bear in mind how, through their humanitarian exertions, members of this small circle of highly educated, cultivated men and women were able to survive the years of barbarism and crime as decent people, free from all brutalisation and indifference, full of understanding and sympathy for all who were suffering, and happy in the knowledge of not having plaintively or despondently folded their arms during those terrible years, but of having struggled for redress with unremitting endeavour and of having fought against the consequences of inhumanity. Then one will not say a single word more about futility. It is said that even years later it was easy to recognise the members of this circle by their expression and by their manner. They spent the rest of their lives as kindhearted, friendly, thoughtful people, never rash, receptive to all that was good and beautiful, averse to all extremes and almost always with a gentle, refined smile on their lips.

The Green Suite

I t had always been there, almost like the blue woollen blanket in the nursery and the golden dots on the wallpaper above the cot. Only, I could touch the dots and the blanket with my finger every day, but not the green suite, because it stood in the drawing room. I was only rarely allowed in there, and never without an adult. What the suite lacked in familiarity it gained in significance, and I can still remember, that for a long time I could never pronounce the words "the green suite", without taking a deep breath before and after.

The green suite consisted of a settee with a raised back rest, two chairs and two easy chairs with curved arm rests, one of which was wobbly and sometimes, if one knew the right rocking movement, could make little whistling noises.

Although I only have to close my eyes to see the old furniture clearly in front of me, I find it difficult to describe their style; perhaps they did not really have a style at all or too many styles. I only know that they were made of curved wood, overlaid with a yellowish brown veneer, which displayed little cracks and faults in several places, and that the upholstery was an elaborately scrolled napped green plush.

One could pull oneself up against these pieces of furniture if one came crawling across the carpet on all fours, and the arm chairs were not too far apart to prevent my first attempts at walking from only just succeeding. My great-grandmother sat in one armchair. She smiled and held out her stick to me for support. Later the green suite was not so large, and it was even possible, if observant adults did not prevent one from doing so, to climb up onto the seat, hold onto the rest and then bounce up and down repeatedly, so that everything creaked and gave off clouds of dust.

But that was not possible if my grandmother was in the drawing room: she seized me by the hand, led me into the middle of the room and pointed, one after the other, at the large gilt-framed paintings on the wall. "Aren't you ashamed of yourself? Uncle Leo and Uncle Max had the furniture for years, and father inherited it — your great-grandfather! — and now *you* are going to ruin it!" And I was ashamed of myself, because I liked the old people on the wall very much. Even if I did not have the fear of them that was expected of me, I did not want to make them sad; and I loved the green suite.

But the green suite could not only be used as a springboard or as raw material for the building of indoor castles or redoubts; no, one could also play with it so silently, that no one outside the drawing room needed to hear; one could be gentle with it, even more gentle than with the two teddy bears and the clown doll.

If one looked at the wood veneer from very close up, it shone and twinkled, particularly on days when Käthe had dusted. In some places, in a suitable light, it was even possible to recognise one's own face, reflected in comically distorted grimaces. If one breathed on the wood, then shine and reflection disappeared, everything turned dull. But after three or four seconds the dull area contracted from the edges again and the wood began to shine as before.

Only if one had breathed very strongly, was breath left behind on the yellow veneer, on which one could then draw with a finger as on a misted window pane. The green plush, which could be stroked like an animal, was good for drawing too. It was smooth and soft, if one stroked it in one direction, and it was rough and scratched like the tongue of the old cat in Gaden, if one brushed one's hand against it the other way. Against the nap its green was darker, so that one could draw on the plush with one's finger, dark green against dull gray; less distinctly than on wood, but the plush surface was larger than the space for the veneer pictures.

Later I was no longer allowed to draw on the plush of the easy chair that could whistle. It had acquired a tear. One of the settee cushions lay on it to hide the tear. If guests came, then my grandmother always quickly sat in this easy chair, to prevent discovery of the secret damage, for whose proper repair money was lacking even then. Instead the damaged chair offered other possibilities. A few gleaming, ornamental, brass-headed nails were loose and one could surreptitiously pull these out, lift off a piece of webbing and look into the dusty interior.

Later still the men from the inland revenue came, made themselves comfortable in the drawing room, carried on cool negotiations with one of the adults, talked about attachment and stuck white bird stamps onto the smooth wood. Then with grandmother's complete approval I was allowed to set to work on the green suite. I was allowed to moisten the stamps and peel them from the furniture, very neatly, so that not a trace of them remained on the yellow-brown wood. "If it was the child that tore them off, they surely can't do anything to us," said my grandmother. As she spoke, she smiled back and forward over the whole suite, because she was not keeping her head still as she normally did.

But they were only plain white stamps; the bird was not painted in colour, but drawn in black. The lettering was straggly. They were not nearly as pretty as the coloured postage stamps which I had begun to collect, but they were stamps nevertheless, and for the time being I stuck them on the final, empty page of my album, because they did not have any post marks. They are not yet used for letters, I had been told.

If I was given white stamps, a few days later I usually had to take grandmother, who even then could not see well, to a little shop in whose windows stray gold teeth lay on velvet, between old coins and tarnished cheap jewellery. It was faded, but it was genuine blue velvet and even softer to stroke than the green plush of the suite. There in the shop grandmother sighed and very slowly rummaged in her bag for objects wrapped in silk paper, then counted the paper money with moistened fingers before she put it away, and always said to me as we stepped out into the fresh air of the bright street: "Another piece less." The green suite remained in the drawing room. I had the stamps, which would have been needed to send it away, in my album.

In 1930, when I was still at primary school, the electricity was cut off. For two years we only had candles and petroleum lamps. I ruined my eyes then, and the green suite suffered from dripping wax. The rare guests were usually told something about a short circuit, and they fell over themselves with assurances that it did not matter at all, on the contrary, candle light was romantic. They usually left early, even before it began to grow dark.

The easy chair that had been creaking and whistling the loudest for years, finally collapsed at that time. It was removed from the apartment. Käthe carried it up to the old junk in the loft, for her it was one piece less to dust. As she did so she sang, "A regiment marched forth from Hungary." But not a single soldier accompanied her up to the loft, only my grandmother slowly followed Käthe, and watched as the armchair staggered higher and higher up the loft stairs in Käthe's hands, flinched, when it bumped against the wall, looked at it once again in its resting place among the old lumber and then stood there uncertainly, as if she should throw three handfuls of dust after it, as she had done for Uncle Dio. Only then did she notice that I had crept after her, and scolding loudly, chased me back down to the apartment.

By the time I went to grammar school, the most pressing debts were paid. There was electric light again and an electric iron. The family made an effort to get the household back to normal. That was when it was decided to let a room. A miscellany of pictures, pieces of furniture and carpets including the green suite, was put into this room. I was not pleased by this, for recently I had won the right to bring my friends, and even a girl I had got to know during the summer holidays, into the drawing room; apart from that, it was sometimes good, if I felt melancholy, to go quietly into the drawing room and, surrounded by the splendour of gilt-framed oil paintings and greenish mirrors, to read some old leather bound volume there. Without the suite, however, the drawing room, despite mirrored wardrobe and rocking chair, was no longer the drawing room. It went against the grain for my grandmother too. She walked continually around the furniture, and afterwards no one could do anything to please her all day long.

But we were not experienced at renting out rooms. After one or two weeks it turned out that our tenant did not appreciate the green suite at all and preferred the dining room chairs. In recent years we had usually eaten in the kitchen anyway, and so we were not very attached to the dining room chairs. However, my grandmother and I dragged the green suite back into the drawing room in triumph.

The girl could come into the drawing room again when she visited me and, as before, I could also recover from the blows of fate on the settee of the green suite. But it did not help against every blow of fate either. When the girl left Vienna, because her parents thought Austria was a country without a future, that things would end up as in Germany, and she went to America with them, I had to bury my face deep in the settee cushions, and even then I did not grow calm, only tired. But when one was tired, it was then that the green plush began to have its effect. It had the dusty aroma of the drawing room and, if one lay on it for a long time, so that the wood of the settee grew warm, there was still a trace of the sharp taste of the long dried veneer glue. Apart from that, in the course of the years the upholstery had picked up aromas and perfume from all the people that had come near it. So one only had to shut one's eyes and could then choose a comforting impression out of all the countless ones there were. That helped too.

After a few years my mother began to be successful with her clothes designs; they brought money into the house. We did not have to let a room any more, and gradually my mother even began to make larger acquisitions. She bought furniture too, a Biedermeier suite, at an auction. She wanted to sell the green suite; it was old and shabby and no good for anything any more.

My grandmother stood in the middle of the drawing room, which looked very untidy because the men had shoved the green suite into a corner and had put down the new Biedermeier furniture in its place. Now the little old woman stood angrily in front of the wobbly plush furniture, each hand clinging onto a chair rest and declared, "The green suite will stay in the house as long as I'm alive. What you do afterwards no longer concerns me."

So the green suite was not sold. It only moved out of the drawing room into the third room in which the tenant had lived. After that I spent more time than before in the third room.

On 11th March 1938 Hitler marched into Austria, on the 24th of April my parents were arrested. During the house search the whole family sat on the green suite, guarded by two policemen. Then I was left alone with my grandmother. We remained sitting there for two or three minutes without saying a word, I stroked the plush. During the house search hundreds of books were eventually taken out of the book cases, leafed through for bank notes and documents, shaken and thrown to the floor. So the room was full of fine book dust, which made the sunbeams falling through the curtains visible, and became visible in them and slowly settled on everything, on the floorboards, on the jumbled, piled up books, on our hands and our hair, on our tongues and in our nostrils, on the plush, on the gleaming yellowish brown wood and in all the cracks and corners of the green suite.

One month later, on the 24th of May, my father was brought home. "Another one less," said one of the policemen. He seemed to expect an answer and looked at the pictures and the furniture. But no one gave him an answer. Then he left again. My father had to be laid on the settee; he tried to smoke a cigarette and lay on the green plush panting and wheezing loudly, until the old family doctor came, gave him a camphor injection and had him taken to hospital. He died the same evening; his stomach wall had been kicked in during an interrogation.

The next day I looked at the settee on which he had lain at the end. I could still clearly see the dirty indentations, where the heels of his shoes had dug into the plush. Otherwise, I don't believe a single person had put his shoes on the old-fashioned upholstery since the days when, as a small child, I had hopped about crowing on the furniture. But it had stood this test well. The indentations could be smoothed out; my grandmother carefully brushed away the street dirt.

When the property manager refused to withdraw the eviction notice he had given, and it became clear that we had to leave the apartment, it was my grandmother who said, ''You will have to sell the green suite too.'' I nodded and looked at her. Her face was calm. ''It doesn't matter any more,'' she said. She was by then over seventy and almost blind. The prisms of the chandelier, which had moved out of the drawing room into the third room with the furniture, reflected the green suite and at the same time refracted the bright sunlight into a multitude of colours and rays, as when one blinks with tears in one's eyes.

One week later a buyer, a metal worker, was found. ''You know, I don't have much money,'' he said to my grandmother, ''but I wouldn't like to take advantage of your situation. You need not imagine, that I agree with everything that's happening now.'' He made an embarrassed gesture with his hand and then offered almost twice as much as the furniture dealer. He lived nearby and took the furniture away one piece at a time, to save the cost of transport. Again and again I opened the doors of the apartment, then closed them behind him and his burden and went back into the room, which became emptier and emptier. The floor was darker where the settee had stood, but on the wall a lighter patch remained. It didn't matter any more, we had to move out in a few days.

Finally, when the apartment was already completely empty, two days before my departure for England, my grandmother insisted on going round it with me, to make sure that nothing had been forgotten. She herself was moving in with two old aunts in another district. Suitcases and old fashioned chests with all kinds of household effects and mementos had already been sent there.

After we had walked through the bare rooms, we went up to the loft. I had to help my grandmother over the last step, which was twice as high as the others. Then, however, despite her poor eyes, she found her way through the lumber better than I did. So she went straight towards the worn out armchair, which rested, where its leg was broken, on a protruding roof beam. She barely wiped the dust from the wood and plush with a cloth and then sat down squarely and comfortably, as if we were sitting on the green suite around the oval table, downstairs in the drawing room. She said, "It's not that bad at all yet." I looked at her anxiously. She smiled.

I had found the missing leg and wiped it. The varnished wood with its curves and little cracks shone in the slanting light which fell through the skylight. In some places I could even recognise my face reflected in comically distorted grimaces, of which it was impossible to tell whether they were laughing or weeping. If one breathed on the wood, then shine and reflection disappeared, everything became dull. But after a few seconds, the dull area contracted from the edges again, and the wood began to shine as before. I weighed the chair leg in my hand. It was curved and looked like an old club or a peculiarly sturdy bone, "the jawbone of an ass . . ." I should have swung the old piece of wood like a weapon and struck, one against Thousands, against police faces and faces roaring approval, against caps, armbands and boots. But I was no Samson. I pulled myself together and suggested to my grandmother repairing the armchair with our neighbour's tools and bringing it on to her. She laughed at me. "Don't be so stupid. You have more important things to do in your last two days here." Then we left the attic.

I travelled to England via Belgium. News came from grandmother until 1942, then she was sent to Theresienstadt and did not return from there. The junk in the loft of the house at 11 Alserbachstrasse burned during the war, when our neighbour on the top floor poured petrol over herself and the apartment and lit it. The damage was repaired long ago, and from the outside the house looks like new. I have not set foot in it again on my visits to Vienna.

"Surrenderedness"

When I was young, still a small boy, this feeling was easy to have. I only had to go to the cinema, which we called the flea pit, a nickname which I thought original and witty and did not yet know to be a generic name, because I did not know that there were more flea pits than this one. So I only had to go to the flea pit and allow myself to be really carried along by the film, in order then, at the moment I left the shabby red cinema behind me together with the sour-sweet smell of the air freshener, which a tarted up matron always sprayed around the cinema with a big spray can, to have this feeling again or, actually, to be had by it, because the feeling was bigger and stronger than I was, and I only accepted it. That this was so, was part of the essence of the feeling, which was one of sadness, disappointment and helplessness at being delivered up to this world again. "Surrenderedness" I called it in my diary, which unfortunately I had to leave behind when I fled, and I considered my word to be an intensification of surrender.

The film would have had to be untruthful and exciting to force me into this feeling of surrenderedness on being ejected from the warm plush into the foggy evening air, which at that time of day also always smelled a little of smoke. Only slowly did I admit to myself, that this very feeling, which hurt me and filled me, not entirely but nevertheless half filled me with fear, was at least as important to me as the visit to the cinema itself, although even the wait in the smoke- and perfume-filled foyer of the flea pit, in which the mysterious love slot machine stood, was always such a memorable experience, that today I still know by heart the poem above the love automat's dial and arrow:

Is her love for you whole-hearted
From your soul can she be parted,
Or does she follow empty fashion
Short on purpose, lacking passion?
Or does she only want your money
While she's up to something funny?
You want to know what will befall?
The Love Machine will tell you all.

I was proud that I could already decipher the fancy writing —
today I know it was debased Gothic lettering. I did not yet have a
sweetheart, but I thought about how many cinemagoers' fates
might well be changed for good or ill by the strict verdicts of the
slot machine, whose arrow spun round after a coin had been put
in and then gave precise information on the character, faith-
fulness or unfaithfulness, worthiness or unworthiness of the
sweetheart. But then the doors of the cinema auditorium itself
opened, the tinkling piano and clouds of disinfectant perfume, as
I called it, seized hold of me, Fox's Movietone News, and then
the film itself wound on, wound off, and I with them.

Only in recent years, five decades later, did I remember all
that again.

And I would probably never have remembered it again, if the
feeling which I used to have on leaving the flea pit had not
suddenly been there again. The circumstances in which it now
appears are quite different. During the last three or four years I
have often been able to identify it, although identification is
actually a presumptuous and dishonest expression, for, of course,
in reality I did not identify the feeling, rather the feeling had
each time taken possession of me again and left me no choice at
all except to acknowledge it. Yes, it was the same feeling as in
those days when I left the red plush velvet seats and the gold
wallpaper of the cinema auditorium, but now it only came if I
had finished reading a book or a story in a book and if the
characteristics of this book or story corresponded in some
respects to those of the old films. However, one can probably
hardly talk about a real correspondence, because the objects of

comparison are too far removed from one another, and besides my knowledge and taste have changed, and my vivid memory of the distant past is perhaps just as unreliable as my hazy memories of what I have only recently read.

And yet I want to specify which characteristics a story or novel must have, in order to arouse the old feeling in me. It must be untruthful, thoroughly unnatural and at the same time demanding, so far as this is somehow compatible with these negative features. That is why I do not experience or suffer this old feeling so very often, because the unnatural and demanding stories are seldom written well enough. There is only *one* writer on whom I can rely completely. He commands the craft of writing just as much as he is commanded by the forces of mystification and pretention. I'm talking about the famous Jorge Luis Borges who, not by accident, enjoys such a high reputation in our complex culture.

At the end of one of his stories, although they portray or sketch quite different surroundings, I can nearly always smell the plush and the sharp disinfectant perfume of my old flea pit which disappeared long ago, hear the tinkling of the cinema piano and the creaking of the poorly oiled hinges of the auditorium doors and see the fancy verses of the love automat in the foyer. It's fortunate that I have never met Borges, otherwise I would have grown too fond of him and would never ever have had the courage to say out loud, that these old memories are almost the only reason I have for loving some of his stories.

The True Borges

It is simply not true, that Jorge Luis Borges never wrote a true word. His statements on official forms and elsewhere about his birth in Buenos Aires in 1899, about his studies in Europe and about his profession as writer as well as about his work as Director of the National Library in Buenos Aires from 1955 to 1973 are, leaving aside occasional small mistakes, such as everyone makes, each one of them true.

True is his love of books, which caused him to fuse and confuse his everyday and everynight life more and more with the life of his literary thoughts and feelings, and also his admiration for South American cut-throats and other action men and his taste for mystifications. It is this last characteristic which lent the ageing man of letters, far removed from the life of the men of action celebrated by him, the reputation of a liar. This reputation is no less justified than the rest of his fame.

Then the question arises, what is a liar. Perhaps Borges — a true Kafka of *artificial* delusions — was no less a victim of them than Franz Kafka was of those delusions which really completely oppressed him. At any rate, Borges demonstrated greatness in mystifying. One could virtually argue that an adverse fate forced the half blind admirer of a world of bright colours, misdeeds and catastrophes, isolated in his libraries, to seek refuge in his imagination and to become such a great liar that one day he even wrote a tale of lies about his own lies. It would be a wasted effort to interrogate a mystifier of his stature, about what his intention really was. Every answer could serve equally well the completion and elaboration of his mystifications as of their disclosure, even perhaps both purposes at once.

So after attentive reading of his works it can at most be

surmised, that in this story his actual plan was perhaps to deceive his own lies to such an extent, that as a result the truth would become known in the end. But because he had long before learned, in his writings, to lie much better than he himself knew, this attempt only made his lies altogether impossible to disentangle.

Yet for him, as a writer who had consciously entered an ever more complicated labyrinth, which he extended with every sentence, this attempt was, in a way, his salvation, because with it he succeeded in achieving again the original miracle of anyone who creates works of art. Because he succeeded, just as he had many years before as a still almost innocent beginner, in achieving the opposite of what he intended.

Small Animal Hunt on the Nile

A pharaoh — like every divine monarch — was already a hero by virtue of his office. It was not, however, sufficient that before the assembled people he placed his foot on the neck of captured enemy generals or kings who had been kept alive until that moment for no other purpose. No, the hunting down of all kinds of beasts from the Nubian lion to the Nile crocodile was also required.

More than one pharaoh can still be seen, on tomb paintings in pyramids and caves in the Valley of the Kings as, from a boat at the edge of papyrus thickets, observed by alert fishes, he thrusts his long spear between the fearsome teeth of a crocodile and deep into its jaws. It can hardly have been without risk.

But although the murals actually had the task of celebrating the pharaoh's heroic deeds, this was thwarted by the manner of rendering homage to the pharaoh which was prescribed by religion. The sovereign always had to be portrayed as much larger than all the people around him, whose size was furthermore graduated according to rank, to say nothing at all of slaves and beasts of burden. In illustrating the crocodile hunt, the obedient artists portrayed the pharaoh, as was their duty and obligation, as approximately ten to twenty times as large as the crocodile.

It is consequently only with difficulty that the ignorant observer can resist the misunderstanding, that the divine monarch was engaged in a lizard hunt, which of course diminishes a little the direct impression of his valour.

Repellent

It is not very surprising that in bad times the truth must appear correspondingly ugly, and that as a result it becomes easy for the smooth lie to appear incomparably more beautiful than the ugly truth.

Now it is true that in looking more closely one would, in time, notice that it is not the ugliness of truth which has such a shocking effect, but only the ugliness of what it cannot avoid showing. Equally, a longer inspection of the lie would gradually discover the cracks and then no longer regard it as so beautiful. But as ill-luck just seems to have it, the first impression at the sight of truth is enough to fill most people with such fear — greater even than aversion — of the ugliness of which they have become aware, that they try to avoid looking truth in the eye ever again.

The bad times, however, which force the truth to appear so ugly, that the decisive, partly silent, partly vociferous majority of mankind would prefer no longer to see it at all, greatly benefits of course, the lies, which are encouraged more than ever, and with them the further worsening of the times.

Nevertheless a comforting rumour is circulating, that several influential and far-sighted lies have recently joined together to call a halt to this development. If one can believe the reports, those lies are said to have recognised that humanity, if it continues to turn away from its true situation, could not only destroy itself, but would simultaneously, of course, also put an end, once and for all, to the lies, for only among mankind and nowhere else can these find shelter, fertile soil and possibilities of reproduction.

That is indeed the pure truth, just as it is true that such a development would not be in the lies' own best interests at all. But just because that is unfortunately true and just because the truthfulness of the lies is after all more than doubtful, it is to be feared that this comforting rumour of the intervention of influential, enlightened lies to save humanity, to secure its peaceful future and therefore also secure the future of the lies is nothing but a lie.

Balance

All that is required is a really large pair of scales. Everything else is simple. The prejudices of a human being are placed on one scale. Dead are placed on the other scale.

With a very open-minded and scrupulous person a few dozen dead are already enough, indeed sometimes, if they are close relatives, even one or two dead people are already enough to balance his prejudices, so that they no longer weigh down the scale.

With most people, however, there first have to be thousands or tens of thousands of dead. With especially convinced and steadfast characters, millions of corpses are necessary, but that is still possible, if the scales are large enough.

Matters get dangerous with people whose prejudices weigh so heavily that there are not enough dead in the world to achieve an equilibrium. Such people can be described as having rock-solid principles.

Neither Fish nor Flesh

Many years ago, when the language of the dolphins had not yet been elevated or degraded to a military secret of the United States, a dolphin of my acquaintance related one of his community's ancient traditions to me.

Almost two and half thousand years ago, in the middle of the Mediterranean Sea, one of his forefathers had heard the last words of the famous Greek Sophist Protagoras, when the latter had been shipwrecked and drowned while fleeing from Athens to Sicily. As has since been reported from Dolphin circles, when the aged thinker — he was then about seventy years old and had been tossed back and forth by the waves like a piece of driftwood — rose still alive to the surface for the last time, he called out the words, "The unmeasure of all things!" Then a foam crested wave struck him in the mouth and he said nothing more.

Although these words of the old philosopher and famous teacher were certainly not intended to be addressed to dolphins, that dolphin swimming past within shouting distance, from whom the tradition originally derives, evidently could not avoid hearing them and simultaneously falling into such deep thought, that he immediately called over several other dolphins.

The thoughts aroused by the words of the wise old man, which had just been heard, also gripped the newly arrived dolphins and immediately led to both lively and profound disagreement among them. Of course, as maritime inhabitants of the waters of Greater Greece, they all knew very well that Protagoras had proclaimed in Sicily and Athens, that man is the measure of all things, of those which are that they are and of those which are not that are not. Consequently an intense dispute had even broken out a little time before, among some dolphins, as to how anyone, whether man or dolphin, could be the measure of those things which are not so that they are not. They had finally allowed this part of the thesis to drift away as all too human. But now it seemed to the dolphins that an abyss yawned between the thesis as a whole and Protagoras' most recent words, deeper than the abyss of the raging ocean, which had already swallowed the aged philosopher and vomited him up again several times. The dolphins, well informed through overhearing the conversations of intellectuals travelling by sea and through reading letters and other writings deposited in their realm by various shipwrecks, at first tended to the opinion that with his exclamation Protagoras had wished to protest against the height of the waves, which truly did not conform to the human measure of things. One elderly dolphin, however, particularly well versed, or perhaps well swum in philosophy, objected that the shipwrecked philosopher could hardly have been concerned with mere externals, no matter how fateful these may have been. Instead his sigh had presumably been intended as a criticism of the behaviour of the Athenians who — far ahead of their times, in this respect as in so many others — had organised a little bonfire of books, the earliest recorded in history, in order to destroy Protagoras' supposedly atheistic, in reality, of course, merely agnostic writings. It was this very intolerance of the Athenian firebrands that had forced the unfortunate sage to take flight, an action which due to the — admittedly equally excessive — storm, had now become his misfortune.

"Might it not be," a young dolphin burst out, "that this man, confronted most forcibly by the superior elements, finally did after all recognise that man is not the measure of all things, a function to which we dolphins are much more entitled?" But he did not meet with much agreement, first of all because human beings, in the dolphins' experience, once they have reached their full length, are no longer capable of learning from experience, but secondly the young dolphin's delphinocentric conception of the measure of all things was also held against him. He was even doing Protagoras an injustice, since the latter had never meant that all things were really shaped according to the measure of man, but solely and simply that man could only comprehend according to his own measure. For that reason alone the violence of the elements could hardly have caused Protagoras to make a recantation.

"Perhaps he meant only, that the hostile behaviour of the Athenians stood in measureless contradiction to the honours which he had previously been granted in Athens and Sicily," suggested one dolphin, and another concurred with him. "After all, on one occasion the great Pericles personally sent him to Thurii with the honourable mission of laying down and recording laws for the town there."

"Protagoras owed his difficulties in Athens solely to the ill-will of Socrates who, supported by Plato, pilloried him as an atheist," said an old, thoughtful dolphin. "Well, we shall see whether Socrates will reap any gratitude for it. Perhaps one day these inconsistent flying fishes of Athenians will treat him in just the same way!"

A dolphin, who pointed out that "the unmeasure of all things" had not been a complete sentence at all, but only a fragment, met with general approval. The first part of the sentence had perhaps been made inaudible by the vomiting up of water, the last part by the wave which had struck him in the face. So one could draw either no conclusions or all too many from this fragment, and it was perhaps more practical to take Protagoras himself on their backs and save him from the waves on which he was being tossed, which would after all, not without justice be counted among the best traditions of delphinity. Then he could personally be asked for the solution to the riddle. All agreed. But when they swam round Protagoras, it turned out that he had already drowned. Of course the dolphins blamed themselves very greatly for having missed the right moment to act with their philosophising, and so not only abandoning the philosopher to his fate, but also depriving themselves, in this case, of the only swimmable route to knowledge of the truth.

Everyone blamed the first dolphin, which had heard Protagoras' last words and hurriedly called them over. He should first of all have saved the unfortunate man and only then called them over, they said. Others, however, objected that a rescue would have required the help of several dolphins to lift the old man up and protect him from the rolling waves. It was a true unmeasure of things to wish now to place the burden of guilt solely on the observant dolphin, which after all had immediately called them to the scene of misfortune. Finally, they held a conference on what they would have done in the place of their philosophical discussion. They did then indeed practise self-criticism, but found their mistake quite comprehensible, hence also pardonable. It was simply that the thoughts aroused by Protagoras' last words had taken hold of them all with such force and intensity because of their real importance that they had been temporarily caused to desist from practical activity. It had been the force of the ideas unleashed by Protagoras which had prevented them from rescuing him in time from the force of the waves unleashed by the storm. This was the tragedy immanent to the case, and it was all the more easily comprehensible since, although human beings' limited power of resistance to the ocean waves was well known to them, it had not become second nature to the extent that the sight of a man being tossed in the water would immediately have stimulated a reflex action in them. For dolphins, only the dolphin was ultimately the measure of all things.

Sadly they all agreed and so contented themselves with calling out their serious disapproval of the irreverent gluttony of two or three sharks which had also meanwhile appeared on the scene and were now swimming away with bloody jaws.

The Real

Let us begin with a relatively harmless hypothesis: Let's say we want to build concentration camps, but proper ones that do not deny their purpose, do not beat about the bush with words of welcome above the entrance like "Work Makes Free" or "To Each His Own," no, extermination camps right from the start, in which the experience of the previous camp builders is utilised as effectively as possible.

So we build our camps, here and there across the whole country, conscientiously, with everything that's necessary: Suitable accommodation for the commandant and his loved ones; pretty little detached and shared houses for senior and junior camp officials; barracks and mortuaries for the prisoners; then, of course, at a not too conspicuous spot, but within easy reach, a solid wall, which can serve as a range-butt for mass-shootings, preferably at the end of a cul-de-sac, between two bare walls, so that escape attempts, particularly by children, who are so good at making themselves small, can be prevented more easily. Not to forget the cells, group cells, isolation cells, cells without light, cells in which it is only possible to stand, special cells, the execution rooms with their meat hooks, the torture chambers and their waiting rooms, the operating tables and the laboratory facilities for vivisections or experiments with fresh tissue material or individual organs. Outside, on open spaces, a few gallows and crosses for public displays, and finally one or two gas chambers together with the necessary furnaces, preferably employing the tried and tested fuel saving method of J.A. Topf & Sons, which utilised the fat of the corpses first brought to firing temperature as fuel for all the subsequent corpses, and which it then had patented after the war in the

Federal Republic (Patent No. 861 731, Class 24d, Group 1, 5th January 1953).

It goes without saying that there are spaces and workbenches for pulling out gold teeth and cutting off valuable hair before the burning of the corpses, for laundering the accumulation of clothes, storage of underwear and shoes, possessions, prostheses etc.

Assuming we all participate, in one way or another, in the construction of these camps, either through our own labour, or by assisting with the necessary technical and scientific planning, or simply because we have, in a democratic manner, agreed the required taxes through our parliamentary representatives and, as ordinary citizens, paid these taxes, then it should be clear to all of us, that we are not guilty of any crime whatsoever. For these camps and purpose-built extermination facilities remain, for the time being, completely empty except for the necessary security and maintenance personnel. They are built solely and simply in case of an emergency, to make sure that if things should ever come to the worst, we have the necessary installations available, in order to deal effectively with our enemies, also with those under strong suspicion of hostility towards us, as well, of course, as far as we shall be able to lay hands on them, as with the wives and children of enemies, and those suspected of being enemies, because this continues to be one of the most effective means of undermining the enemy's morale.

Yes, even assuming that, to be on the safe side, we build not only the minimum necessary number of extermination camps, as calculated by our statisticians and planners, but twenty to forty times that number, with all the requirements, from bone-mills to well-furnished villas and apartments for the administrative and supervisory staff — carefully screened from the camp itself and surrounded by flower beds — then we are not guilty of any extravagance. Not only are we creating innumerable jobs at a time of unemployment, a truly creative kind of work moreover, in which the worker sees the product of his labour, the barracks, places of execution and flower beds literally growing out of the ground, we are merely complying with the demands of human caution and forethought. The great number of these camps, twenty to forty times the minimum requirement as ascertained by experts, is after all nothing more than a fundamentally reasonable precautionary measure to ensure security — or even revenge — for ourselves and our dependents, should the enemy actually succeed in deliberately and ruthlessly destroying the greater part of our carefully prepared installations, and the national assets invested in this labour, in a cunning surprise attack. Thanks to the multiplication of our construction activity, we would, even in such a tragic situation, still dispose of a sufficient reserve of extermination camps, so that the enemy who had fallen into our hands would not, in reality, be helped at all by the orgy of destruction directed against our camps, and this could perhaps even deter him from an attack.

In our hypotheses, we would of course have to reckon with the irrationality to which some people fall victim. It is inevitable that there would be isolated extremists who would rebel against our work. We would have to expect their propaganda tricks and demonstrations, even, unfortunately, acts of violence. In this case, it would have to be seriously considered whether we did not have the right, in fact the virtual duty, to forcibly provide such law breakers and violent criminals with a more useful role, by turning them into test persons, on whom the effectiveness of our new facilities could be tried out even before the outbreak of an emergency. At any rate, the great majority of our fellow citizens will certainly refuse to allow themselves to be disturbed any longer, even by such violent criminals and their no less guilty friends and accomplices, in the achievement of the great task we have embarked upon.

The task itself, the construction of comprehensive extermination facilities in the manner of our fathers and grandfathers, at first appeared to us to be a playful hypothesis, as it were, seemed perhaps even inappropriate and a little artificial. It would, however, be unjust for us to regard it in this way. The proposition that we all co-operate in the construction of a series of extermination camps is a training aid. In just the same way we can first get to know and understand a complicated machine, which we will subsequently have to use ourselves, from a simplified model.

Those fundamentally quite harmless camps from the time of our fathers and grandfathers, whose operations are still easily discerned, were very familiar to us long ago from many stories, reports and photographs. They seem almost homely, like everything that is familiar and so are very suited to stimulating our imagination in a modest way and to preparing us on a small scale for much more comprehensive present and future tasks and for their consequences, which are still far from predictable. For it is no mere hypothesis that the great majority of the population would refuse to allow itself to be disturbed in the common effort of preparing extermination facilities in case of an emergency, with the taxes it pays, with its professional knowledge or with its physical labour. No, it really refuses to allow itself to be disturbed and it really is preparing extermination facilities.

For some time we have all in fact been supporting — directly or indirectly, thanks to all kinds of agreements — a much more ambitious programme of such installations than that of all earlier generations. In reality, of course, these are no longer the obsolete concentration camps, which, if dirt cheap, were also all too limited in their destructive capacity, but our modern facilities, which virtually deny any future at all, and which we are preparing today in case of an emergency. These are our new methods of exterminating the enemy, weapons with which we subordinate matter itself — together with their firing and storage apparatus, their bunkers and silos, their co-ordination and command centres equipped with every necessity for survival and long-distance killing, not forgetting the bacteria and viruses which are to be employed afterwards.

Of course, compared to the extermination camps of our fathers and grandfathers, these installations have a crucial advantage, for in those days the people whose elimination had been decided first of all had to be caught, assembled and then brought to the extermination facilities in troublesome ship-ments, which could not be accomplished without hardships bordering on cruelty. But our methods from the start exclude capture and laborious transportation, which also makes them suitable for far larger quantities of people. We no longer have to manage the transport of the people to be eliminated, but only the means of their extermination. The people themselves will then simply be exterminated on the spot, with unprecedented effectiveness, possibly in their own homes, without prior painful separation from family and friends, without deportation and transportation involving unavoidable humiliation and ill-treatment, and will for the most part also be simultaneously cremated.

Let it be noted that in our preparations for this step we in no way make ourselves guilty of any crime, not least because according to reliable information from our civil service experts, the enemy in question is preparing very similar facilities for use against us.

Naturally, the harsh reality in which we live demands immeasurably greater sacrifices from us than the old idyllic extermination camps. The necessary expenditure of taxation revenue alone is today already of a quite different order from even the building of twenty to forty times the number of extermination camps regarded as necessary. For unfortunately, just as in our mental exercise we built forty times the required number of extermination camps originally held to be necessary, in order to avoid frustration of our plans by the enemy, so following the rules of so-called overkill provision, we really are forced, for security reasons, to have available twenty to forty times the minimum necessary number of weapons, rockets and rocket silos.

On the other hand, however, the quantity of dead which we can achieve, and even guarantee, with our new armaments and re-armaments, is incomparably greater than the total perform-ance, in this respect, of all the extermination camps from the time of our fathers and grandfathers.

There is no need at all to mention here those who will not be dead immediately, or the manner in which they shall spend the last weeks, months or years before their death, although our facilities, in this respect too, leave not only the achievements of our predecessors, but also their boldest fantasies, so far behind, that in comparison to the potential of our present provisions their fenced-in camps were mere child's play.

What was then begun modestly and in all secrecy can now be described as having reached its full development. Unlike the planners of the extermination camps of those days we also no longer need to fear the light of publicity. What today is planned for an emergency, is known — at least in its principal features — to everyone, or could be known to everyone who wants to take an interest. Thanks to a programme of popular education by schools and the media, concerned on the one hand to enlighten and on the other to reassure, divert and wholesomely amuse, our undertaking receives, if not the active, then at least the passive approval of the overwhelming majority of the population, and so only a small radical minority seriously tries to object. It, however, is so small, that in an emergency it will be child's play to eliminate it once and for all.

Københavens Amts Sygehus Gentofte

Amts Sü-hus. But the letters are different. There are *more* letters. On the sign it's Sygehus — with a Y. As so often in Danish, the middle syllable is swallowed. Amts Sygehus. One doesn't have to speak Danish to understand it. Amts is Amt — office. The Office is the district office, or simply the district. The district of Gentofte, which was a village before Copenhagen grew large. A village with an Amtmann, a district official. Sygehus means sick house, so Copenhagen District Hospital Gentofte. Sü, written syge, in English "sick" is an old word for being ill: Sicken. Sicken unto death.

Here in this big, semi-darkened room no one is ill. No one is sickening unto death. Here there is peace.

Peace. Never before can one have known so well what peace is.

Many years ago, in an unexplored stalactite cave, one's lamp fell out of one's hand and was extinguished. Then it was dark. No difference, whether one opened or shut one's eyes or after a while opened them again. This calm now is like that: No difference whether one breathes or stops breathing, whether one listens or whether one doesn't want to listen to anything any more, whether one looks or doesn't look.

As a child, if one woke up in the morning and was ill and at first felt nothing, other than that one's hands were heavy and awkward, one believed that overnight the fingers had grown thicker. If one clenched one's fist, each movement of the fingers seemed to last a very long time and somehow to reverberate, just like an echo, at the very end, when one can no longer hear but still feel it. It is like that now with looking: The eyes have become heavier and it takes a long time, and then somehow there's a reverberation. It's not that the light is too weak. No, the man who opened the doors to the semi-darkened room, must have switched on a light in the room. No searchlight, but bright enough.

Only the face. The face and the hair. The face and the hair and the neck and the shoulders and arms wrapped in white. And the hands. Nothing else, but that is everything.

The face and the neck, framed and enclosed by a kind of white lace collar. Not really lace. Cheap material or even paper. Uncertain, whether material or imitation. Uncertain and infinitely unimportant. But very white and very old-fashioned.

The women, who really wore something like it, must already be dead a long time. If that means anything. If one can be long dead. If there is *long* and *short* with that, if one can be more than simply living or dead. Be dead. Is it really possible to say then "one is dead"? or "A man is dead"? Or a woman or anyone? Or *is*, or *was*, or anything at all apart from *dead*?

And is the face still a face? Beside me, in the semi-darkness, the man, who knows me, with whom I have come here, says, softly but quite clearly in English, "I don't feel that this is still *her*."

He does not have the feeling that it is still *her*. One hears these words and understands them, and they don't concern one. The voice is clearly audible, but the peace has not been interrupted. If one had not heard it clearly, or not *everything* clearly, or if one had heard but not understood it, if one had perhaps not understood the language, then it would have been a noise. Then it *would* have disturbed the peace. But the noise of the words has become absorbed by their meaning, and the meaning has become absorbed by something else, as one looked at the face. The meaning doesn't concern one any more.

So this human being can no longer be a human being. So this face can no longer be a face. But this face is a face. This face is entirely a face, that one knows and that one will know, as one has never known it before.

This face is and is and is. There is nothing, that *is* just like this face, there is nothing, that endures like this face, although one does not even know and cannot say, whether the eyes are open or shut. Although one does not know and cannot say, whether it had become sharper or softer than it was, finally or earlier or much earlier.

This face is this face, and the shoulders are these shoulders, and these arms and these hands *are* these arms and these hands, the arm and the hand on the other side, and the arm and the hand on this side, the hand with the finger that wears a ring. And a voice, which earlier asked at the door, who one is and whom one wants to see, now asks, whether the ring should be removed. And the other voice, which one knows and which had spoken English and said, "I don't feel that this is still her," now says in Danish "Nej," and one answers with him and shakes one's head in the semi-darkened room. The ring is *not* to be removed.

There are some things which are, yet are not. There is an attentiveness, which is not attentiveness. There is a looking about oneself, which sees nothing, which believes itself to be utterly peaceful, and which is perhaps as restless as nothing else can be, and really wants nothing except to avoid a face, or which at least wants to see something else apart from this face, and apart from the shoulders and the arms and the hands and the ring on one finger and the old fashioned white lace collar. There is an attentive taking in of all the details of the semi-darkened room, which simultaneously is *not* so, because afterwards one will not even know any more, whether there were steps or not, and whether there were benches and stools, and whether there was a second light. There is a not wanting to see this face, although there is nothing except the still wanting to see this face. There is a peace and a dignity, which is not peace and dignity. For the peace and the dignity of a dead person is not peace and not dignity, just as it is not without peace and not without dignity. It is there just as little as the sky is there, which is only the empty space above the empty air. And yet the sky, which is not there, is there, and the peace and the dignity, which are not there.

The peace and the dignity of the dead. That's nonsense. Every stone lies as peacefully, every piece of wood, every discarded bottle. One could just as well grant peace and dignity to the open coffins as to the dead who lie in them. That's true. But that it is true does not affect one. Nonsensical peace and dignity is still peace and dignity. Peace and dignity like nothing else. Someone has said the dead only decay because nature cannot bear their peace for long. That too is nonsense. Nonsense of the same kind. If the dead did not decay, then there would be nothing that would be so enduring and so real as the dead. Then everything would be different. Then one could get used to the dead and would not have to part from them. Then one would not have to say, that is no longer them at all. Then one would *have* the dead around one every day and use them, as one has and uses household things, pieces of furniture. Then they would be there in the room and in the kitchen and on the landing and in the garden, then they could sometimes be a support for bookshelves or for lamps, or for eaters and drinkers or for lovers, or they could lean against the wall in the nursery, so that no child would have to be alone and be afraid of falling asleep. Then the dead would be there just like the living, who could then not constantly forget that they die, but whom the dead would relieve of the fear of death. That is all nonsense.

The others are gone. Only the face is there, and the white lace collar is there, and the shoulders are there, under the white material, and the arms and the hands, and the ring on one hand is there, and that, which does *not* look like an open coffin. But nothing is there as the face is there. The face, which is the face that it no longer is. The face that will always remain that face and that one sees, as one has never seen it before, although one does not even know, whether its eyes are open or shut, and although one will never know that either now.

The face is larger, because it is nearer. Above the face there is a forehead with short hair. This short hair one touches with one's lips and smells with one's nose. It smells as it smelled before. Nothing has changed. The hand with the ring is larger because it is nearer. The hand with the ring is large and one touches it with one's lips. Nothing else, but that is everything. Everything is peaceful. Everything is as peaceful as nothing else is.

The voice which asked whether the ring should be removed is there again. A pair of scissors is there, and one takes them. Two or three very small tufts of hair are cut off and placed in an

envelope, which came together with the scissors. On the
envelope stands:

Københavens Amts Sygehus
1 Gentofte
2900 Hellerup

At some time one will forget these words. But now one wants to
forget, that one can forget.

The envelope is stuck down and is put into the wallet that one
is carrying. No remembrance, but a wish to throw something
away. A wish from this face, when this face was not yet as it is
now, when it still spoke words. Words, that not *everything* should
be burnt and buried here in this country, if it is to be in this
country, but that *something* should be in another country and
thrown away there, scattered, in England, down in Sussex, at a
spot in the open country. At a spot, which this face liked to see.

It was perhaps difficult for this face to express such a wish.
Questioning words had followed immediately after the wish,
whether such a thing could be desired, whether such a thing was
not stupid. Now this face no longer expresses any wish. But now it
has not been difficult to do such a thing. Now it has not been
difficult, to cut off the hair and place it in an envelope. And now
perhaps it will not be difficult, to take it to England, to the spot
down in Sussex, and to scatter it. That's simple. As simple as
giving milk to a small child which is crying.

The face above the lace collar saw small children and spoke to
them, as they stopped crying and drank milk. It was not yet *this*
face, but *yet* it was this face.

The man, who brought the scissors and the envelope, who
asked about the ring, who opened the doors to this semi-
darkened room and switched on the light, is there. He is there
and looks at one. He is there and accompanies one to the door.
The light is still shining on the face. One goes out. Not alone. The
man with whom one came here, whom one knows, the man who
said "Nej" to the question about the ring, comes outside too. But
the man who switched on the light and asked about the ring, has

not come outside. He has remained in the room, which through the half-open doors looks darker than before. The doors close from inside.

The Stork

Some memories go back to my earliest childhood, when I could not yet walk. Doctors, who questioned me a great deal during my first school year and then talked to one another about it, called it incomplete childhood amnesia. Since then I have discovered that many more children than one would imagine have such early memories. But adults usually persuade them that they are only repeating what they've been told later.

My great-grandmother, who had lived with us, died when I was one year and three months old. Immediately after her death the furniture in two rooms was moved around. But later I could describe exactly where this furniture had stood before the death of my great-grandmother, whose voice, face and black clothing I can still remember very well. Pieces of furniture were important supports for me, to keep me from falling over while learning to walk. Sometimes they were impediments which could trip me up, for example the protruding feet of the sideboard, which were carved as bird or lion claws. I can still also remember today the card table, which was sometimes an obstacle, but sometimes also a support, like the shiny black stick with the carved, yellowed ivory handle, which my great-grandmother held out to me for my first attempts at walking, as she was sitting firmly in her armchair. It helped me to stay upright, if it didn't just happen to get between my legs. By describing this stick and the original position of each individual piece of furniture my memories were finally given credence — even if not the very earliest ones, from the time when I was still in my pram.

One of my most important experiences, shortly after the death of my great-grandmother, is also connected with a piece of furniture, a footstool. I was not quite one and a half years old and could only walk clumsily, although apparently already talk quite well for my age. In contrast to my many pronouncements about the furniture, I never discussed this experience with my mother or grandmother, although it was very significant to me and is also my first memory of a thought process, of a relatively complicated and at the same time painful reflection.

When I was a year and four or five months old, a footstool was often pushed up to the kitchen window for me, a solid old piece, dark brown, with round curved legs. Once I fell as I climbed up, after that I was supported or my arm was firmly held. Then, when I was standing at the open window and reached just as far as the window sill, a lump of sugar was put in my hand, which I was supposed to place on the window sill for the stork. I was also taught a rhyme:

> Long-legged stork,
> Bring me a brother!
> Long-legged stork,
> Bring me a sister!

Whenever I had placed the sugar on the window, my grandmother, sometimes also my mother or the maid, pointed out to me that the sugar was no longer there. The stork must have taken it.

But then, despite these encouraging preparations, nothing happened. I remember from this time lying on my mother's bedspread in an unfamiliar room, and twisting off one of the toggles which fastened the cover to the blanket. But my mother wasn't cross and only stroked my head. I did not know that this room was in the Hera Sanatorium, where I had come into the world too; neither did I know that this time my mother had given birth to a dead child there.

During the days and weeks that followed I did not stop asking after the stork, although I no longer received any sugar, and I also asked, as well as I could, after the brother or the sister which the stork was supposed to bring me. But both my grandmother and my mother responded to my questions with incomprehension:

"Brother? Sister? — What are you talking about, my child?" I pointed at the footstool, which still stood in the kitchen, and repeated the stork verse which I had been taught.

"No, my child, we never said that to you. You must have dreamt it." The maid too only shrugged her shoulders.

I still remember very well my complete bewilderment. I only need to close my eyes, and then I see my grey-haired grandmother and the maid with her brown plaits rolled into a bun on the back of her head, and the white painted window frame. It was a double casement window, but unlike the windows in the drawing room, dining room and bedroom it had no window bolster. There was only the bare scratched window sill, on which I had placed the sugar. But had I really placed it there? And the stork poem? Had my grandmother recited it to me or not? I did not yet know words for lies or hallucinations, and yet I thought something which could perhaps be put into words like this: "Either I am not what I believe, or they are all telling me something that is not true."

At that moment I saw the scar above my right knee. On the second or third occasion, when I was supposed to place the sugar on the window, I had fallen from the stool and had cut my knee. After that I had been firmly held or supported each time and I had not fallen again, but the scar was still there. It was a quite different colour from the rest of my skin.

I took a deep breath and looked at the scar. I touched it with my finger. It could not be wiped away and was smooth and soft. I didn't say another word and did not recite the stork verse either. Neither did I point at the scar, as I had previously pointed at the stool, but I knew now that everything was as I knew it to be, and not as my grandmother, my mother and the maid had told me. After that I as good as never believed adults unhesitatingly, not even years afterwards.

Wunderkind *Time*

In Liechtenstein Park, the only park close to the apartment house in which I lived four flights up, I discovered that I could not run and jump as well as other children. I was not surprised at this, because my father had already frequently reproached me for it, at the same time expressing doubts as to my ability to survive, before finally indulging in reflections on how a man like him had come by such a child.

These reproaches upset me more than my clumsiness, for which I nevertheless had to suffer later, thanks to various gymnastics teachers. But in the park I had hit upon a simple way out. I gathered other children around me and explained to them that for a change we would, for once, not jump over string and run races, but do something else. Then I told them exciting stories, which I usually had to make up very quickly, or we put on some fantasy comedy or tragedy that I had thought up. Naturally I took a part as well.

I attracted the attention of an unemployed theatre director named Hans Wachsmann, who wanted to be famous, to which end he had given himself the stage name Hansmann and roamed the park scouting for talent. He took down my address and persuaded my mother and even my grandmother to let me take part in a Raimund production. (Raimund was a popular Viennese playwright of the Biedermeier period, whose works even I already knew from the puppet theatre.) A troupe of children, most of them, however, much older than I, were to perform Raimund's *The Spendthrift*, unpaid, at a number of theatres in and around Vienna, for the charitable purpose of erecting a statue to the great Raimund actor Girardi. We were then also to undertake a number of professional tours.

Grandmother and mother gave their consent. When I developed into the star of the group, my mother supported my new career of *Wunderkind* enthusiastically. On the whole I felt very pleased, because I found learning parts just as easy as acting and my successes on the stage made up for my clumsiness at sport.

One of the successes was that even the older children of the group fully accepted me, in addition there were laudatory newspaper reviews, admiring glances from friends and acquaintances, but also the huge bonbonnières and bouquets of flowers, which were brought up to me from the auditorium at the end of a performance. Once I even received an indoor palm, which, however, to my considerable regret, soon withered.

There was one terrible misfortune from that time, failure would be much too mild an expression, which I forgot so completely that only as a grown man did I remember it again. At my mother's instigation I had just finished reciting poems and monologues before a large circle of relatives in the house of a rich uncle, when to the great delight of the onlookers I suddenly wet myself. The hysterical laughter of the aunts in the room and the derision of some of the male onlookers were so unbearable that even by the day after my hasty retreat I could no longer think about the details and after a few days had again recovered to the extent of regarding my artistic career solely as a chain of unbroken successes.

Certainly there were sometimes hitches too. For example one evening the unfortunate make-up girl had to stick on the grey beard and the tangled grey-white hair, which went with my role as a beggar, at least four times. One of the mothers had brought a small child, who was frightened by the grey-white mass of hair, into the dressing room. I therefore tried to make clear again and again — by pulling off beard and wig — that I was a child too, and there was no need to be afraid of me. My attempts to comfort the crying child finally brought the make-up girl almost to tears. But when I was called onstage, the beard was at last stuck on properly, only the wig was a little crooked, but no one noticed that.

Things weren't quite so simple with the newspaper reviews either. These were certainly very flattering to me, especially since they were written in the inflated style of Viennese reporters of those days, but it had occurred to my mother that I should learn the reviews off by heart. Even that was still tolerable, but then she called upon me on every possible and impossible occasion: "Go on, Erich, say what the newspaper wrote about you."

As a good child I then said: "As 'Azur' and 'Beggar' Erich Fried was not only a brilliant speaker, but also an actor of extraordinary demonic effect . . ." But I had my own opinion of the word *extraordinary*, which I considered to be almost synonymous with *extravagant, too much of a good thing*. So I emphasised the first two syllables and said each time: ". . . *extra*-ordinary demonic effect . . ." and each time my mother kicked me under the table or prodded my back, and if no one happened to be too close, hissed in my ear, "You stupid boy, how often do I have to tell you, it's ex-tra-ordin-ary?"

I found this recital of newspaper reviews at my mother's behest embarrassing, and not only because of the secret rebukes. I found it much more gratifying that Hansmann, our director, evidently seemed to need me. I always had to be present to speak to the journalists at press conferences before the performances. He praised me: I could talk like a book. Altogether he liked to show me off, certainly with greater skill than my mother, but gradually it became clear to me that I was important to him, so that he could make a name for himself. That gave me a self confidence, which otherwise I would have sadly lacked, even almost a sense of power.

That stood me in good stead during a so-called professional tour by part of our troupe outside Vienna itself. At night in the hotel two of us were always put in one bed for reasons of economy. At supper in the Hotel Panhans in Semmering, I declared that I would only play my part tomorrow, if tonight I was put in the same bed as Erika. I was passionately in love with Erika who, at twelve, was exactly twice my age. I got my way. Erika, somewhat embarrassed, but clearly also flattered by the feelings of the star of the troupe, consented and declared, "You can hug and kiss me, but otherwise you must be a gentleman." I promised and also held to it, although I had no very clear idea of what a gentleman was.

While falling asleep I firmly resolved to dream of even more intense caresses. This wish too was fulfilled, but as an endless nightmare, in which Erika and I were two rhythmically moving skeletons.

The next morning in the breakfast room, as we ate, with such an appetite that I was no longer even annoyed at the skeletons, Erika sat on one side of me and on the other a Hungarian boy of my own age, Szandor, also in love with Erika. He was not a star, however, and consequently could not win a place at her side, still less in her bed. Szandor had returned my morning greeting sulkily. When breakfast was almost over, he had suddenly disappeared, and immediately afterwards I had felt a strange sensation on my left thigh. I looked under the table and then pulled a somewhat embarrassed Szandor up by the collar. He had tried to cut off my left leg with the breakfast knife; this, it is true, was made a little easier by my short trousers, but was, nevertheless, a completely hopeless undertaking. I was not even bleeding. His motive was clear to me immediately, yet I also had sufficient imagination to sympathise with him. Shaking my head I asked him, "How can you be so stupid as to believe that I won't notice, if you do it without local anaesthetic?"

Only a few weeks before a sore finger had been cut open at the hospital using local anaesthetic, and now I thought I knew everything there was to know about local anaesthetics. Szandor, however, did not want to enter into any discussion, but looked me straight in the face and said "Baah!" which shocked me and made me feel infinitely superior to him. Not until many years later did I have doubts as to whether his reaction had perhaps not been the only appropriate one.

Six months later, however, at Christmas 1927, my sense of self confidence on stage, acquired through my starring role, had quite different and, I think, better consequences.

In that year, 1927, in Vienna, right wing radicals who had

murdered workers in the village of Schattendorf, had been acquitted on each and every occasion by judges who were closer, politically, to the murderers than to their victims; despite a large demonstration by outraged workers, they were ultimately acquitted again on 14th July 1927 by the Supreme Court, which sat in the Palace of Justice. On the following day police and demonstrating workers clashed. One policeman was killed, but the police shot eighty-six workers.

By chance, my mother had gone with me that day to the First District, the city centre, and because the streets were no longer safe after the beginning of the fighting, we had found shelter in a shop belonging to acquaintances. Through the shop window I saw stretchers with dead and wounded.

Shortly afterwards the writer Karl Kraus, who lived in Vienna, had big posters put on the city's hoardings, addressed to Police President Dr Schober, who was responsible for the massacre: "I call upon you to resign — Karl Kraus," ran the text. As far as I can remember, the words *you* and *to* were placed one above the other in the layout, which made a deep impression on me; I had only recently learned to read and was quite unable to write properly yet. Bloody Friday, as the day of the massacre was called in Vienna, was, of course, the adults' subject of conversation for weeks.

My first school year was 1927. My teacher had discovered my ability to declaim poems, all the more quickly since I made no secret of it at all. Now at Christmas I was supposed to recite a poem in the hall which my Marktgasse school shared with two others in a nearby community centre. As I was already standing onstage, I heard someone below say, "The Police President is also among the guests." So I stepped forward, bowed, and in my best speaking voice, said, "Ladies and gentlemen! Unfortunately I cannot recite my Christmas poem. I have just heard that President of Police Dr Schober is among the guests of honour. I was in the city centre on Bloody Friday and saw the stretchers with dead and wounded, and I cannot recite a poem in front of Dr Schober." I bowed once again and then stepped back. The Police President, whom I only now saw, jumped up and immediately left the hall, followed by two or three companions. He or one of his entourage slammed the door shut with a bang. I stepped forward again and said, "Now I can recite my Christmas poem." I declaimed the poem, which as I now know, was in any case pitifully bad, with all the pathos I had been taught. Loud applause, I bowed again several times and then left the stage. My teacher, Franz Ederer, a left wing Social Democrat, was already waiting for me. He embraced me, "That's wonderful, Erich. Where did you get the idea from?"

My father was less pleased. He growled, "I won't put up with it. The boy is floating about in Communist channels!" I had no idea what that meant, but since my father, who had also been against my acting activities, said it so dismissively, I concluded that it must be fundamentally a good thing. Apart from that I loved my teacher, whereas I was at that time constantly and not quite without reason angry with my father. So I was keenly interested in what he had said and decided to find out what his words meant as soon as possible.

We did, it is true, have the de luxe edition of Meyer's Encyclopedia, but unfortunately only the first six volumes, so that the word GAIMERSHAIM was the last one. Volume 6 did not even go as far as GESCHLECHTSORGANE — sexual organs — never mind KOMMUNISMUS. So I could only look up FAHRWASSER — channel. There it said: "The deep part of a river, harbour, strait or estuary, where the current or tide is strongest; passage which ships have to navigate in order to reach their goal safely."

For the other word I had to wait until the next time my grandmother took me to Aunt Anna, who did not have the de luxe edition, but did have all the volumes. There I looked up KOMMUNISMUS, and also, thanks to the constantly repeated reference "op. cit.", Socialism, Marx, Engels, Socialist Laws. So I owed my first introduction to the basic elements of political science to my father and an edition of Meyer's Encyclopedia from the turn of the century.

The Great Day of Linz

"Have you still not had enough?" asked my grandmother shaking her head. "How long have you been sitting by the radio?" We, my father and I, had been sitting there for hours already, and listening, listening, listening. The whole day, in fact. We had enough, more than enough, but we couldn't tear ourselves away. And what else was left to us, except to hear what was happening? We had become, at least for the moment, entirely passive receivers of history, suffering it. It was the 12th of March 1938. Austria had ceased to exist the evening before. That too had begun for us on the radio, with the voice that had announced the end: "Austria is now faced with a difficult decision. The government of the Reich has delivered an ultimatum to the Federal President . . ." And so on to the concluding words: "And so I take my leave of the Austrian people with a good German saying and profound wish: God save Austria!"

That was followed by the Austrian federal anthem, the final bars of which finished very slowly and sadly on this occasion. The speaker of this valediction, Federal Chancellor Kurt Schuschnigg, who just like his murdered predecessor, Engelbert Dollfuss, with his clerical three-quarters fascism, had paved the way for Hitler, without perhaps himself realising it, had now said in his brief speech: "I state before the world, that the rumours that workers are rioting, that rivers of blood have flowed and that the government is no longer in control of the situation, are completely invented. We are yielding to force."

These words alone were good enough reason for the new rulers to imprison him for years. The producer of the broadcast paid for the instruction to let the anthem end as slowly and solemnly as a funeral march with a few months in a concentration camp.

Immediately after the anthem, martial music had begun, and an announcement of who the new federal chancellor appointed by Hitler was, who had to effect the homecoming of the Ostmark to the Reich. Then Nazi songs again: "Storm, storm, storm, storm, storm, storm ring the bells from the tower . . ." Later in the song appeared the words: "Juda comes, to win the Reich." And as a challenge to that: "Deutschland erwache, Deutschland erwache!" (Germany awake) which rhymed with "Rache" — revenge — in the next line.

It had gone on like that day and night. Now we were listening to a live broadcast from Linz, the capital of upper Austria, which was expecting the triumphal entry of the Führer, Adolf Hitler. The men at the microphone, in part local Nazi bosses, were looking out over a large square, on which Hitler Youth and BDM girls, as well as thousands of sightseers were assembled. They also informed us that candles were ready in the windows of most houses, to be lit at the Führer's approach, but that the Führer's arrival had been delayed. It was cold and everyone was waiting impatiently.

The fact that some of the Nazi bosses had evidently been drinking heavily occasionally lent the commentary an odd quality. So one of them shouted out, "It's cold. The knobbly knees of the Hitler Youth are wobbling in the wind." To that he added the rousing call to the Hitler Youth: "So now let's sing the song about the world quaking." But it was far from being about the bones in the shivering legs of the Hitler Youth, because the song that was struck up, went:

> The world may quake in feeble error
> One bloody war has put it straight.
> We have smashed through every terror
> The victory for us was great.

> We will march forward together
> Through all the uncertain hours
> For Germany we have today,
> Tomorrow all the world is ours.

The last two lines were repeated. The actual text, composed by a Hitler Youth member called Baumann in fact ran "For Germany hears us today,"* — but the Nazis *had* got the words right. I heard them for the first time that day and have never ever forgotten them. In fact the text demonstrated the talent of its author, since the formulation that the Nazis owed their victory to the fear of Communism on the part of many powerful people in this world, whose bodies had quaked with fright, was altogether true to the facts. The falling apart too was not so far fetched and was to become even more true in the future, not ultimately, however, the expectation of victory.

Meanwhile the time had come: the drunken voice at the microphone bellowed, "The Führer is about to roll up! Light up all the houses!" He did not mean, however, that Linz should destroy itself. The man had only meant to say, "Light all the candles," but was no longer sober enough. The short interval until the arrival of the Führer was filled with eyewitness reports of how penetrating and magical the Führer's gaze was. A subsequently famous Nazi, who was to become notorious as a war criminal, stood at the microphone: "I was once presented to the Führer, but the Führer took me for someone else, so I said to him, 'My Führer,' I said, 'the real Doctor Rheintaler from Linz that's me, that's me! me! me!' " In the end his bellowing had grown louder and louder, so that he was still audible as he was courteously removed from the microphone.

But the gentlemen were not too drunk on this March evening to be able to do harm. They were still reporting with emotion how nicely the candles were shining in all the windows, when one said, "Except over there, it's dark in Pick's house." "Yes," said a second, "Pick is picky!" and then, in a voice that was supposed to imitate a Jew who spoke German with an accent: "Well, of course we won't pay for a light!" General laughter rewarded this performance, but it was immediately followed by an earnest warning, please not to underestimate this Mr Pick. "They were

* "Denn heute hört uns Deutschland" rather than "Denn heute gehört uns Deutschland". [trans.]

still loading up weapons from his house yesterday. For Vienna. They were heard shouting 'Long live Moscow'."

My father and I looked at one another. Whoever this man Pick might be, things didn't look good for him, and the next voice was already saying, "Well, then we'll have to go over there and take a closer look!"

Now we had really had enough. The Führer's entry into Linz didn't interest us any more. The business with the weapons was, of course, just as crude a lie as the assertion that someone had shouted "Long live Moscow". That was the picture of the enemy the Hitlerite shouters had. And the weapons for Vienna were part of the fairy tale about rioting workers and rivers of blood that Schuschnigg had already formally denied. But at the same time we knew that this man Pick was completely helpless at the mercy of this drunken horde. Any lie was good enough to destroy him.

Years later I talked to a Catholic clergyman who had also heard this radio transmission from Linz. During the night he had then prayed for Pick the Jew. Neither before nor after did he or I ever hear anything else about him.

My Heroic Age

The word hero was already suspect to me at secondary school — or, as we called it in Vienna — at the senior gymnasium. It had the ring of false military pathos, and it smelt of blood and putrefaction. The words heroic age, however, which were also part of the vocabulary of our teachers, were not yet contaminated for me at all, and I even asked myself whether every person, who wants to develop fully, must not have his own heroic age. There was also a little of Winnetou and Old Shatterhand* going round my head and with "every person who wants to develop fully", I was also, of course, thinking about myself. It is true that Bertolt Brecht said, "When I hear that a ship needs heroes for sailors, I ask whether it is rotten and old," but I did not know these words yet, even if I later understood why he longed for times and communities that need no heroes.

My own heroic age, if it can be called that, began on the 24th April 1938, and ended on the 5th August, when I left the border of the German Reich behind me. But it can only be called that, if it is understood as a time in which heroism was simply forced upon me. Besides one cannot really call such a short period of time an age, and since I only turned seventeen during this time, it would perhaps be more appropriate to call it my heroic youth, a perhaps even more insufferable phrase, but one that is at least unquestionably comic.

On 24th April 1938, my parents had held a big meeting with many acquaintances in the Café Thury, which was on the ground floor of our apartment block. The subject under discussion was how to make the departure of several close friends

---

* Characters in the adventure stories of Karl May. [trans.]

and acquaintances financially possible. I had annoyed my mother with a few sceptical remarks on the risk of such a large meeting in a coffee house, now that the Nazis had been in power in Austria for six weeks. There could be no question of risk, she said, I should come downstairs myself and listen to everything. "No thanks," I had said, "someone has to be left if you all get locked up." I had also asked my mother for a couple of hundred marks so that, in case they were all arrested, I would have money for a few days and to find a lawyer and buy food for my grandmother and myself. She had given me the bank notes unwillingly and said, "If we really are arrested, then they'll find the money on you too!"

Then she had gone. By now she and my father really should have been back for more than an hour, and I began to grow restless, although I explained to my grandmother and to myself that in these times one was simply nervous for no reason at all. At the same time I was still expecting a loud knock at the door to our apartment.

It happened differently; only the familiar quiet sound of the key in the lock, the door opened and my father was there. I had not been so happy to see him for a long time. But my happiness only lasted a second or perhaps even less, because another man stepped in behind him, in plain clothes, but identifiable at first glance as a policeman even to me. He looked at my grandmother and myself and said, "House search."

My father and I had to go from one room to the next and always be in the room in which the search was taking place. The police officer conscientiously took hundreds of our numerous books from the open or glass fronted book cases, held them with the spine facing upwards, opened them wide, ran his fingers through the pages, to see whether bank notes or something else of interest to the police was hidden there, and finally let the whole book, still open, spine upwards, fall to the floor, onto the carpet, onto the floorboards or onto the last book that had been dropped.

At first my father, an old-fashioned book-lover, had twitched every time a book fell, but after a while he no longer showed any reaction. The police officer, on the other hand, began to lose patience. "What've you got so many books for?" he rudely asked my father. "If my wife were to bring so many books into the house, I'd have thrown her out the window together with all the books a long time ago." My father looked at him, then nodded in agreement and said, "I can very well imagine that."

Now it was the policeman's turn to become thoughtful. Did these words mean something offensive, under the cloak of agreement, or were they simply after all acknowledgement of his manly strength of purpose? He evidently decided on the second assumption, for it might almost have been possible, as he looked at my father, to have taken the wobbling of his fleshy face for a smile. I on the other hand, had to clench my teeth together, in order not to laugh out loud, although I felt like crying. That was my first heroic deed.

My grandmother stood or sat there without batting an eyelash throughout the whole house search in each of the many rooms of our apartment. Life only returned to her face when the search was over, though nothing was discovered, as it happens, which, however, did not help my father and my mother much. The hundred-mark notes, which I had hidden in the fuse box for the electric light, had not been found either.

When the door had closed behind the police officer and behind my father, whom I had quickly embraced and kissed, the first time in many years that I had done so spontaneously, my grandmother said, "They should all drop dead." She meant the police and the whole Hitler regime. She, who could usually be characterised by the epithet 'the eternal grumbler', had made do with five words. Then she had helped me to put the books lying on the floor back again.

During the days that followed my heroic deeds followed thick and fast. But they were all mini or micro heroic deeds, like my not laughing at my father's joke, the last one I heard him make. They were heroic deeds, which probably not a soul apart from myself would have recognised as heroic deeds, but which nevertheless helped my self confidence greatly.

The next heroic deed was to call a lawyer in Germany, Dr

Günther Weiss, an old Nazi and friend of Rudolf Hess, from a public telephone. My mother, however, knew him from Germany, and he had saved a Jewish architect and his wife, Bruno and Käthe Kalitzki, friends of my mother.

My mother had told me a lot about him, including the fact that he was bitterly disappointed by the Nazis. I had to make sure that he would understand on the telephone who I was and what was at stake, but without giving away information which would immediately allow me to be identified or which incriminated me if the call was being tapped. How could I start? I knew a lot about Bruno Kalitzki and I knew that the lawyer knew that my mother was an interior designer. So when he replied, I spoke into the phone as casually as possible, "Good afternoon, I'm calling from Vienna. I am the son of the interior designer, and it would be good if you could come here quickly. It's one of these Bruno affairs."

He understood right away, and he also, which impressed me enormously, had a Lufthansa timetable on his desk, so that he could immediately tell me when he was going to arrive the next day. I was to pick him up. He also, not without some irony, gave me a brief description of himself.

The next two heroic deeds, even before his arrival, were necessary inquiries as to who, apart from my parents, had been arrested. Mrs Markus was a key figure. She lived nearby. It did not cross my mind to call from a telephone box some distance away, but instead I put on my most child-like short trousers, and with them a rowing top, as we called it in Austria in those days, a kind of T-shirt. I decided to leave an old childhood coat, which I also wanted to put on, at home after all, despite the cold wind. I put an egg in my pocket and made my way to Mrs Markus. At the door to the apartment I held the egg in my hand, took a deep breath and rang. A plain-clothes man threw open the door, snarled at me, what did I want. "Good afternoon!" I said. "I only want to return the egg. And thank you very much!"

"Give it to me!" He grabbed the egg and threw it to the ground so that it burst, with a sharp crack. "Now see that you clear off," he said to me and slammed the door shut. I knew what

I wanted to know, but for a moment I stood there, half paralysed with fright, not because of the smashed egg, but because it suddenly occurred to me, how easily it could have been the same plain-clothes man who had carried out the house search at our apartment. Then the trick with the egg would not have helped very much, on the contrary.

The next heroic deed, about an hour later and this time no longer without the fear of falling into the hands of the police officer who knew me, but nevertheless full of hope that the man whom I was now going to see had not been arrested at all, was a visit to the apartment of a Mr Klein, a younger, very likeable person. "I shall be pleased to see him again. I want to ask his advice," I said to myself.

And I did see him again. He looked likeable, only a little pale, but I could not ask his advice, and I wasn't pleased either, because he came towards me on my way up the staircase of his house, accompanied by two plain-clothes men. He passed me without giving any sign that he knew me. I simply climbed further up the stairs. After only a few steps I had reached the floor with the door to his apartment. It was open, a plain-clothes officer had one foot outside the door and was looking down at his two colleagues with the arrested man. I climbed up the next flight of stairs, but it was the last one. What was I to do, if the policeman remained standing at the open door? I dared not arouse any suspicion. On the doorframe of one of the doors on the top storey was a so-called Mesusah, a small parchment scroll bearing a Hebrew motto on the inside which, according to ancient law, pious Jews must affix to their doors. I had never had much time for such customs, but now I was relieved and grateful. I rang the doorbell, asked to come in briefly, and explained the reason for my difficulty. A little disapproving, because I was going around without anything on my head, which offended against the religious laws, I was allowed to wait in the apartment for a couple of minutes and agreed on the excuse that I had come to the wrong address because of a mix-up of names. Then I went down the stairs again. The door to the apartment of the Klein family was shut. Again I knew at least part of what I wanted to know.

The next heroic deed was, of course, meeting air passenger Dr Günther Weiss at the airport, because I was afraid that I had perhaps after all aroused the interest of some spy and would be arrested on meeting the lawyer. I even had my eye on a particular man who, as I waited, walked up and down, exactly in step with me, and looked at me from time to time, apparently with impatience. Was he waiting to arrest me together with Dr Günther Weiss? There was already some kind of regulation which was supposed to make it difficult for, or even prevent, lawyers defending Jewish clients in criminal matters. That the man was also simply waiting for someone would in itself have seemed possible to me; but the thought that he could simply imitate my walking back and forwards out of sheer nervousness, did not occur to me. Only when my lawyer appeared did I see this man embrace and kiss a woman who had also just arrived.

The German lawyer proved to be as resourceful as he was humorous and understanding. Both my choice of words on the phone and the manner of my researches visibly amused him. I quickly came to trust him and also passed on to him, in addition to an exact report on my parents' case which, of course, contained more than the authorities knew, the documents I had so far accumulated in preparation for my own departure. An exit permit, especially if like me one also had to get hold of a passport, was no simple matter at that time. A tax certificate of non-objection was required and several other documents which I cannot remember at all any more. However, a lawyer from the so-called Old Reich, Germany within the borders of 1937, could make procurement of them easier, especially if he was a party member.

I had regular discussions in the following days with the lawyer, who reported to me on the success of his efforts day by day and who, apart from that, had begun an affair with an aristocratic acquaintance of my mother. He seemed to have a soft spot for the name Grete, I said to him. I knew that he had also taken a very decided fancy to Grete, the wife of the architect he had saved in Germany. He grinned at me: "You really are good at research."

During those days I indulged in the deceptive and pleasant feeling that Dr Weiss would manage to take care of things, and there seemed little occasion for heroic deeds. At most a postcard to my mother in prison might be mentioned. I reported on the fate of our dogs: "Czibi has stayed with us and is still barking and growling like mad. Foxi is with our neighbour, because I can't look after both, and Schnuffi is with Aunty Hermine." But Schnuffi was in reality not a dog, but the nickname of my mother's friend, and Aunt Hermine, my mother's aunt, lived in Holland. So my mother learned that her friend was beyond Hitler's reach.

Unfortunately it turned out that there was still occasion for heroic deeds. It began with Dr Günther Weiss proudly telling me about a small heroic deed of his own. He had given a Gestapo official, who did not want to put him through to an office in Dresden, a piece of his mind, because he had lost patience with his bureaucratic fuss and finally shouted at him, "What are you there for, you mule?"

I was not very pleased. "If you talk to these people like that, then I could perhaps already be visiting you in gaol on Tuesday. But I'd better send Grete, that's safer and less compromising for you." We both laughed. But then I did ask him about his good connections, which could perhaps be useful to him, if anything ... "Don't worry! It will come to nothing, they won't dare touch me," he said. He was evidently amused by my fears for him. "My only connection here in this odd little country, which has now simply come home to our blessed Reich," he said, "is Dr Wölfel. I made friends with him at the gaming club on Sunday, more precisely, after the club."

I was impressed. Wölfel and Dr Führer, as the other was appropriately called, were the two leading Nazi lawyers in Vienna. I knew that Dr Weiss had a weakness for games of chance. I had even, for that reason, revealed a system for roulette to him, by which I set great store, but which of course I had only tested on a toy roulette. By pure chance he had won a large sum of money the previous weekend using this system, which I learned long ago was no better than most other so-called systems, and generously given me 5,000 marks of it and in addition declared all his legal fees covered.

We were supposed to meet on Tuesday morning, but he didn't come. A phone call to the hotel yielded the reply: "Dr Günther Weiss is no longer staying here. Two gentlemen took him away this morning." I called Grete and asked her to go to the hotel and investigate. She was pale when she came back. He had been arrested. She did then visit him a couple of hours later, but could not speak to him alone.

The situation was to all appearances fairly bleak for me. Not only my exit papers, but also my confidential notes about my parents' case had been in his briefcase. I could either wait until this report was read, then they would take me away too, or I could try to cross the border illegally without documents. I would probably be arrested or shot in the act, since I had less than average physical skills. Apart from that, several others, either already arrested or not yet arrested, would have to bear the consequences, i.e. they too were even more threatened than before by my confidential report, if the Gestapo were to read it.

There remained the possibility of managing to get the report back from the Gestapo unread. To attempt this was the next and at the same time the first almost really heroic deed. Except for a few marks, I gave Grete all my money for safekeeping, declared who was to be informed in the event of my arrest and who could possibly take the case over, as well as which relatives could look after my grandmother, all far from optimistic instructions. Then I laid out my childrens' clothes ready to put on, so as not to be caught up in a possible round-up of Jews on the way, quickly took a bath, put on fresh underwear, to make the most favourable impression in case of arrest and also to feel more self confident, added a towel and a piece of soap to the various documents in my briefcase and set out for Dr Wölfel, the leading Nazi lawyer.

The waiting room of his huge chambers was full of waiting SS men, who looked at me with surprise and, so it appeared to me, with hostility. If I had thought more carefully, I would have been less alarmed, for presumably there was not a single one of those waiting there who had not himself got involved in some crooked business and needed legal assistance. The unhappy expressions on their faces probably had nothing to do with me.

After a very long time it was my turn. Dr Wölfel, far from being a bellowing fanatic, had urbane manners. "Please sit down. What brings you here?"

"Dr Günther Weiss, whom you recently got to know, is in trouble."

"What kind of trouble?"

"This morning he was arrested at his hotel by two gentlemen."

Dr Wölfel looked at me in surprise. "Is it a civil matter?" he then asked, his eyes twinkling. He meant the crime of race defilement, which had only existed in Austria for a few weeks.

I allowed myself a very brief laugh. "No, the lady he is friendly with is a baroness, pure Aryan." I gave Grete's full name.

"You seem to be well informed?" asked Dr Wölfel amused. "What do you think has happened?"

"Dr Weiss had an argument with a gentleman from the Gestapo," I said. "I think it concerned a Jewish client in Dresden. The official was not willing to help Dr Weiss in some way, and Dr Weiss finally lost his temper and shouted at him: 'What are you there for, you mule!' I believe the affair is an act of revenge. Dr Weiss told me that to have Jewish clients is not always looked upon with approval. And that plus insulting a civil servant . . ." I didn't finish the sentence and looked straight at Dr Wölfel. I knew from Dr Weiss that Dr Wölfel also took on Jewish clients for appropriate fees and that therefore a precedent in which a lawyer with good connections, known to be a party member, could be arrested because of such a matter, would not be welcome to him. Dr Wölfel whistled through his teeth. He then said, "I must first ascertain if this is correct. To do that I must make some phone calls. Do you first of all wish to supplement your information in any way?"

"Yes, I would. Dr Weiss also mentioned in the conversation with the Gestapo that he is on good terms with Rudolf Hess."

"What, and despite that . . .?" exclaimed Dr Wölfel.

"Yes, evidently. And something else. In his briefcase there are also eight documents relating to the arrangement of my departure from the country, as well as a confidential report by me about my parents' case, which Dr Weiss is also dealing with. Since Jewish clients are *also* involved here, it would perhaps be in the interests both of Dr Weiss as well as of my parents and not least in my own interests, if these documents could be retrieved before they are dealt with."

The lawyer scrutinised me, then he said, "I'm beginning to understand why Günther Weiss discussed his affairs so openly with you." Then he briefly asked me about my parents' case and subsequently led me into a tiny waiting room that had no window, but only artificial light. "I must make some phone calls now," he said. "It will take a little time."

There were magazines lying in the waiting room, but I didn't have the peace of mind to read. The similarity of the small windowless room to a cell was too great. I knew, admittedly, that Dr Wölfel did not owe his status as a leading Nazi lawyer to fanatical party activity, but to the circumstance that four years before he had been one of the two lawyers defending the Dollfuss murderers, Planetta and Holzweber, who after forcing their way into the federal chancellery and shooting the Federal Chancellor Engelbert Dollfuss, who was widely disliked and not just by National Socialists, had been arrested and hanged after a dubious trial. But even if he owed his party position principally to his activity as a lawyer, these were nevertheless very questionable people I had got involved with, and also there was no sign that the National Socialists had now become as repellent to him as they were to his new friend Günther Weiss.

His politeness towards me could be pure professional practice. Presumably he would make his first call to the Gestapo, although he had also asked me for the number of Dr Weiss's chambers in Germany and for his private number. It was far from certain who would be standing at the door of my little room when it opened again. In my thoughts I once again paced down the long corridor from Dr Wölfel's office to this room. The space left to walk through had been very narrow, because, just as before, right along the corridor from the large waiting room to the office, old paintings and wood carvings had been leaning against the wall and sometimes even against both walls. I had heard from Günther Weiss that Wölfel also accepted art works instead of cash payment from imprisoned Jewish and other clients whose bank accounts were frozen. A mixture of treasure chamber and robbers' cave, I said to myself. At any rate the cave of a species of civilised robber who were also art experts. Well, I had to go on waiting.

The door opened. No, not plain-clothes men who had come to take me away. Dr Wölfel stood in front of me.

"I called up Germany and then also made local calls here in Vienna. All your information was correct, and unfortunately also what you surmised. I shall try to do what I can for my friend Dr Weiss. But it will not be so simple."

"That is very bad," I said. During the few days, I had developed a liking for Dr Weiss. I looked at Dr Wölfel. "I would be terribly grateful to you, if you could help him," I said, and added, "insofar as my gratitude can mean anything to you. His behaviour to me has been unbelievably decent."

Dr Wölfel placed his hand on my shoulder. "*Your* case is much simpler. Can you come here tomorrow morning at half past nine?" I answered in the affirmative, we shook hands, and I went home. The next day at nine o'clock on the dot, I presented myself at his chambers.

Again the waiting room was full, again partly with SS men. But this time I was taken first. Again I went past the piled up pictures and wood reliefs into Dr Wölfel's office. But he was not alone. "Good morning," he said. And then, turning to the other man in the room, "District Director,* this is the young man whom I've told you about." The man who had been addressed stood up and held out his hand. "Pleased to meet you," he said. This person was therefore evidently not waiting to take me away, as I had feared for a second. "I have some documents here for

---

* i.e. Bezirkshauptmann: district administrator in Austria. [trans.]

you. Would you please acknowledge receipt of them and sign this piece of paper?"

On the piece of paper was only the date and underneath the words, 'I confirm that I have received nine documents.'

I counted. Eight documents were papers relating to the arrangements for my leaving the country, the ninth was the confidential report. I signed, watched benevolently by both men, and drew an oblique stroke through the lower half of the initial letter of my first name as I was in the habit of doing in those days.

"Is that a secret sign?" inquired Dr Wölfel.

"Of course," I said, "it's a very dangerous Communist conspiracy. Both men laughed. "Well, young man, the best of luck in your future life. Goodbye."

I expressed my thanks and took my leave and in a few seconds was out of the door and out of the building and on the way home with my documents.

The joke was, that the oblique stroke through the first letter of my name really was a secret sign. Because I had founded a sort of underground movement, only eight or nine strong, and this was the way we always reminded ourselves of our membership. That this secret society, the inexperience and romantic naïveté of whose activity corresponded exactly to this secret sign, was not detected, and that we all survived, seems to me now in retrospect almost a miracle. But that is another story.

These heroic deeds or follies, as well as everything else which happened before the end of my heroic age or my heroic youth, that is until the day of my departure for England, pale for me in comparison with the retrieval of the documents confiscated by the Gestapo, although that too really seems quite simple when one tells it now.

My father died about two weeks later as a result of an interrogation, as I recount in another context. My mother was sentenced to five years, but was released thirteen months after her arrest and just before the outbreak of war came to England, where she lived to a great age.

Dr Günther Weiss remained in prison for a long time, even

after my departure for England and, grotesquely, he encountered the greatest difficulties after the war because of his earlier infringement of the rules applicable to lawyers in Bavaria, where he lived. This, although *impenitent* former National Socialists had by then long been carrying out their functions as lawyers, public prosecutors and judges; in fact perhaps precisely because of that.

I helped him after the war as much as I could with statements and even returned the money which he had given me, appropriately revalued. Unfortunately he died shortly after he had succeeded in rehabilitating himself as a lawyer.

The remaining heroic deeds, should I remember any, can be left to another occasion.

My Resistance Group

I do not think I can remember anything else in my life in which a certain degree of courage, realism and sense of responsibility was combined with so much frivolous, childish romanticism, impossible to justify under the circumstances of the time.

A few days after Hitler's entry into Vienna, in the second half of March 1938, I invited a few school friends round, like myself all Jewish, and founded with them a resistance group, whose members all not only swore silence unto death against the Nazi authorities, but also agreed that each one of us must add an oblique stroke to the lower half of the initial of his first name, running from upper left to lower right. The motion of one member that each of us should also cut our arm and drink a blood brotherhood was rejected by a majority. We thought we were too grown up for that. No one had any objection to the stroke through the initial letters.

At that time most Jewish families were subjecting their book cases to strict censorship. Treasonable literature, especially Marxist books, were removed and destroyed, for they rightly feared the worst, if these books were found in their apartments. The tiled stoves of the old Vienna apartments were going at full blast.

I had of course read about the book burnings in Germany, and I grieved for each book. The principal task of the resistance group therefore consisted of visiting all our Jewish friends and acquaintances, vividly describing to them how dangerous it was, now that the winter was really over, still to be burning paper all day long, which smelt and could possibly be noticed from outside from the rising smoke. It was much better to give us these books. We would take them to people, non-Jews, who hated the Nazis and needed just such books, in order to have reading and teaching material against them. Only the ex libris, names and rubber stamps which could betray the origin of the books would, of course, have to be removed.

Since the destruction of their books was in any case painful for many book owners and others regretted the burning or it seemed to them to be too dangerous, we received enough books, sometimes more than enough. We did not want to carry them in large suitcases. We rightly considered school bags and shopping bags to be more inconspicuous. Also, we all learned that books in any quantity are not at all light to carry, and if we had not been trained in carrying by the pack marches of the para-military training forced upon us in the immediately preceding years, the accomplishment of this self-appointed task would have been even more difficult for us. We brought the books to people whom we knew to be Socialists or Communists. Due to our very imperfect knowledge we also made a few little mistakes. For example we took a whole number of books by Leon Trotsky to a Communist family, loyal to the party line. They were then presumably burnt even more quickly than would have been the case in the Jewish homes.

The illegal propaganda material which we had typed on our typewriters with lots of carbon copies weighed considerably less than the books. We did not know that it is possible to identify typewriters by their type just as easily as handwriting. None of us had a clue about criminology.

The typed material partly consisted of extracts from works like Leonhard Frank's *Man is Good* or Nicolai's *Appeal to the Europeans*, but partly also of elevating poems, which I had usually composed. I still remember with a sense of shame the refrain of one of my poems, which we distributed:

> Arise! for man ascends the heights!
> Above repression and all hate
> His step is godly, proud and free.
> To make men happy is our fate
> While those who suffer grief still wait
> For us — march too, then you shall see!

Even the beginning of this poetical work was not much more of a threat or more concrete than this refrain. It ran:

Need and hunger, war and hate
Rage upon this earth,
And so we call upon you all
To witness a new birth.
Lead people to some better state!
Give hope to those who sadly wait!

However vague these slogans were, if we had fallen into the hands of the Nazis, the numerous copies of such verses in the pockets of Jewish schoolboys would have been enough, not only to expose us to serious ill-treatment, but also to put us in a concentration camp. The Hitler regime only had sympathy for youthful high spirits when it suited it.

We had not taken any precautions like, for example, putting on swastikas before we collected and took away books or pushed our propaganda material through letter boxes or under doors. Not that we would have scorned disguising ourselves with swastikas. The idea had just not occurred to us at all, no more than we had realised that the construction or even purchase of a simple duplicating machine would have been far simpler than the constant typing of propaganda material.

So it happened one day, as my friend Edmund and I were walking along Liechtensteinstrasse, our pockets full of propaganda material, that we got into difficulties. Near the entrance to the Strudlhof Steps we saw an SS man standing on the street and looking at us. We changed, inconspicuously as we hoped, to the other side of the street, along which ran the wall of the Liechtenstein Park. But an SS man was standing there too, and he stopped us.

"Are you Jewish? Austrian citizens?" We truthfully assented to both. "Come with me." We knew that this did not mean anything more than that we were to do the cleaning in some SS barracks or other. It would have been unpleasant, it is true, and one had to be ready to suffer a few kicks or blows, but that would not have been so serious. However, we also knew that in recent weeks the emptying of all pockets and the inspection of their contents had been added to this ritual, and in our case that would clearly end badly. It was as good as certain, that I, who anyway had a slight disability and could not march well and not jump and run at all would not survive a stay in a concentration camp. So this is what death looked like? A middle-aged man with a somewhat melancholy but far from vicious face, whose little red broken veins on nose and cheeks indicated, perhaps, that he drank too much.

I pulled myself together and asked the SS man very seriously. "Is it absolutely necessary?" I looked him full in the face and he looked at me and my friend. I don't know for how long, but probably it wasn't longer than a second. Then he waved his hand and said, "You can go." I said, "Thank you very much indeed," and we went. After we had taken a number of steps, Edmund asked me, "How did you do that?"

"I don't know, just come away." Our courage for this day had disappeared without trace. We searched for the nearest public convenience, and both of us, without having said anything to the other, were not content with leaving the propaganda material in the lavatory cubicle, no, we flushed it away, although the repeated flushing must have been more obvious than if we had simply left it lying.

Later, after the arrest of my parents, I had less time to devote to my resistance group and after a few years of exile I had as good as forgotten it. Not until twenty years later did I meet Erwin Schön, another former member of the group, who forcibly reproached me for my forgetfulness. For him belonging to this more than a little childish secret society was one of the decisive experiences of his life. The difference, as he called it, between simply being spat on and secretly hitting back.

The Unworthy Families

Which of the persecuted Jews ended in Hitler's gas chambers and which obtained a foreign visa in time, before the outbreak of war, depended not only on chance but very often on which social stratum they belonged to. Certainly, however, it was also sometimes a matter of chance. Anyone who had emigrated to Belgium or France or even found refuge in Czechoslovakia or in Italy, was overtaken a few years later by the lackeys of the Hitler regime, unless he was hidden or could flee further. Among those who were caught up later, there were also, of course, the affluent who had originally had no difficulties in obtaining a visa and residency permits thanks to their connections and foreign assets.

Usually, however, especially in Germany or Austria, it was the poorer, in particular, among the persecuted who no longer got out in time and who were, in the end, deported and exterminated. They were workers and unemployed, who were often not very familiar with how to get hold of documents or correspond with foreign countries. They were the old, to whom the far from hospitable host countries usually only granted visas if they had enough money, so that there was no risk that they would become a burden to the host country; and finally they were the orphans.

At the time there were many children who had lost their parents, among them complete orphans, e.g. where the father had died in prison or in a concentration camp and the mother had committed suicide on hearing the news. It is true that Jewish orphanages and communities concerned themselves with the emigration of these orphans, but in general things went much less quickly and effectively than with children who still had parents or came from well-to-do families.

I had until then only encountered orphans in the fairy tale books of my childhood years, and although, since the murder of my father, I myself was now half-orphaned, in the autumn of 1938, as a penniless, seventeen-year-old refugee just arrived in London, I had other worries than wondering whether such a definition applied to me. Apart from that I no longer felt myself to be a child. But a series of grotesque coincidences made it possible for me to help get a few orphan children to England out of Hitler's reach.

Edmund, a school friend from Vienna, now a refugee like myself, had obtained a minor post in the Bnai Brith Committee for Children. Bnai Brith was a kind of Jewish freemasons' lodge and concerned itself with children of the Jewish faith, while the Quakers tried to bring the politically or racially persecuted of other religions e.g. Christian children of Jewish origin, to England. This division of labour had the purpose of making sure that none of the saved were unintentionally estranged from their religion. However, it diminished the effectiveness of the relief work.

The Bnai Brith Committee was accommodated in a large old house on the edge of Bloomsbury, number 150 Southampton Row, and my friend Edmund's immediate superiors were three attractive young women from wealthy Anglo-Jewish families who carried out this work as a kind of charitable duty, perhaps also in the hope of one day receiving some kind of honour for it.

Meanwhile they attempted partly to beautify their office, partly to make it more homely by bringing objects from their own domestic surroundings. So one had brought along, apart from a few solid pieces of furniture and embroidered cushions, her dog, the second her cat and the third a number of potted plants — dog and cat of course only in the day time.

Now, astonishingly, dogs and cats generally get along much better with one another in England than they do with us. This dog, however, a dachshund, and this black cat, were an exception. They couldn't stand one another. As a result a large part of the energy of the three young ladies was spent in preventing the dog and cat doing any harm to one another or damaging the potted plants during their chases through the committee rooms.

Of course the work, of which there was in any case more than enough, suffered because of it. On the one hand, the mountains of applications for places for children, who at that time still obtained a visa relatively easily, if families could be found who wanted to take them in and who could prove that they were in a position to guarantee maintenance and education. On the other hand, however, there were long lists of families who were willing to receive children. Edmund knew these lists, for he had to type each of them three times, "because it looks better than carbon copies," it was explained with a smile.

In those days there was not yet any vaccination against poliomyelitis, infantile paralysis, and there were many people whose children had died. So among the married couples who had registered their willingness to accept children, there were many who had lost their own children and now usually wanted to take in a child of the same sex and of the same age.

A computer would have accomplished the bringing together of these two groups, the orphaned children on the one side and the prospective families on the other, in a matter of seconds. But computers did not exist yet, and punched card methods, which had already existed for a long time, were unknown to the three young ladies. Nevertheless the work could have been managed, had not the dog, the cat and the flowers claimed a large part of the working day of all the office staff.

This not only led to delays but also to disagreeableness. Minor incidents, such as the notice that there was no need to be bothered about this or that child any longer, it was already dead, caused dismay for the moment, but no further interruption of office routine. If, however, after many weeks, a family which had declared itself ready to take in an eight-or nine-year-old girl, received the information, "We now have a twelve-year-old boy for you," then the applicants were dissatisfied, and not only refused to sign a guarantee for this boy, but possibly even took the liberty of asking whether a nine-year-old girl could not have been found among the great number of those being persecuted and in need. Then one of the committee ladies would reply: "That is not your concern, please leave that to us."

So then there were angry telephone calls with mutual accusations, and the result was that Edmund had to draw up some new lists, not as lengthy as the others, but nevertheless still quite considerable: Lists of families, which because of their discourteous behaviour towards the committee were not deemed worthy of being allocated a child. "Such ill-mannered people would not be good for the children." That death in the Third Reich would also not be good for the children evidently did not occur to these young ladies. I knew all this from Edmund's stories; I would often come to the committee rooms to meet him after work, or for a very long lunch break, which we liked to spend in the British Museum, which was very near, and so on more than one occasion I had been witness to the differences of opinion between the dog and the cat and the resulting threat to the pot plants.

Edmund had for some weeks owed me the enormous sum of ten shillings, one half of a pound sterling. In those days that meant a week's rent for me or also, with the most careful choice of shops, a week of being able to eat.

However it was very uncertain whether I would ever get the money back. So it was no great sacrifice for me to offer Edmund an exchange. He did not need to give me any money back, if he was prepared to copy out for me the lists of families who, because of their lack of respect towards the committee, were considered unworthy of having a child allocated to them. But, as on the original lists, he must always note the wishes of these families, especially the sex and age of the children they were looking for.

Edmund, who was by no means overburdened with work and had long ago lost interest in the never-ending scraps or the menacing growling and spitting of the two animals, had nothing against making up these lists. Even before I received them, but when I already knew I was going to get them, I wrote to Vienna and asked friends there to collect, very quickly, photos and ages of children in the Jewish orphanage who wanted to come to England. My lists were, of course, much shorter than those of the committee, the children concerned were fewer too, although in the end my friends did not restrict themselves to one orphanage in Vienna. So it was easy for me to find photos and age specifications of children which fitted the wishes of the families rejected by the committee. I now went to see these families, one after the other, showed the children's photos, and after a short conversation nearly always got to the point where they really were willing to take in the children. However, their willingness to co-operate with the committee was no greater than that of the of the committee ladies to have anything else to do with them.

This difficulty had to be overcome. I went to the Quakers, I put the case to them, related how the disagreements had come about and explained to the somewhat worried Quaker ladies that I was far from interested in a scandal, but only in the children, whose only chance this was. Also, no alienation of the children from their religion was to be feared, since the lists themselves were originally drawn up by the Bnai Brith Committee. It was only a matter of the Quakers agreeing to deal with these cases of children of Jewish faith as an exception.

The Quaker committee conferred briefly, and I received a positive reply the following day. I heaved a sigh of relief. In my eyes, separation according to religion in such rescue work was in any case only troublesome pedantry.

A few weeks later the children really had reached their unworthy families. I do not know whether the three young ladies learned about it, but I don't believe so, otherwise Edmund would have got into trouble. I had emphasised to the Quakers that this must be avoided.

In my enthusiasm for the task I did not notice that I too had only dealt with a small part of Edmund's lists. I had not visited families outside London, because I had too little time and money for that. Neither did I have enough energy to write. The idea of looking for like-minded people, who could take care of the remainder of the lists, and who could even ultimately request more cases from Germany and Austria, did not occur to me at the time, at seventeen years of age and still without any connection with emigré political circles in London.

The Commission

I received my first commission as a writer when I was eighteen, in London, a few months before the outbreak of war. Mr Berg, son of a well-to-do family from Germany, and after several years already familiar with exile in London, had talked to me for an hour. He explained to me in his somewhat sharp manner and in a language in which the native Berliner was obvious, although it was free of any Berlin accent, "What will become of you remains to be seen. For the present you are not yet a writer, still less a poet, but a little piece of shit." And after a benevolent glance at me, he added, "A very small piece of shit." I was shocked and firmly determined to prove as soon as possible to this man, who was less than ten years older than myself, that I was a poet, or at least a writer.

Berg sat opposite me in his comfortably furnished apartment in Hampstead, dressed with casual elegance. He had offered me a cigarette, but I didn't smoke. He had offered me a whisky, but I didn't drink. Neither increased his respect. On the contrary, he only shrugged his shoulders suggestively. So *that's* what a writer looked like who was already successful despite emigration, for Berg had contacts with some fabulous film company.

"Can you write film scripts?" No, I could not do that. Yet again a shrug of the shoulders, as with the cigarettes and whisky at the outset.

"I can make you an offer. You have told me about your family, how your father was killed and that your mother is still imprisoned. It doesn't need to be a film script. You only have to write the whole story down, truthfully and in complete detail, typed, of course, then you will receive fifty pounds."

I turned red. In those days I could live for half a year on fifty pounds. Apart from that, for the first time in my life I now had a literary commission. It could hardly be difficult to write down truthfully the story of the destruction of my family. I had all the details in my head, in fact I was quite full of them and I felt compelled to talk about them again and again. I wanted to start that very afternoon; I couldn't wait.

"There's another two pounds on top of that for paper and expenses," said Mr Berg at the end of our discussion. He shook my hand and came to the front door with me, silently, on his thick crepe soles. His attractive secretary watched us. I greeted her as well. I envied him for his house, for his typewriter, for his secretary. I was certain that she was also his lover. Her admiring glances already showed that. Only much later did I realise that Mr Berg had no interest in women whatsoever.

Then outside the door it occurred to me that I did not have a typewriter. My typewriter had been left in Vienna. I walked past two or three typewriter shops, but even the cheapest model, second-hand, with only three rows of keys, cost three pounds. Apart from that it was doubtful whether I could write at all on such a machine, with only three rows, on which one constantly had to move a lever back and forward. The question was academic, since I only had two pounds and ten shillings in my pocket, even counting the two pounds from Mr Berg.

Already somewhat at a loss and dejected, I again found myself standing in front of a typewriter shop with the sign: "Entry free. Take a look at our stock. No obligation to buy." I went in, a smell of oil, spirit, ribbons. Typewriter upon typewriter lay there, all far too expensive.

Suddenly I saw one of the shop assistants carrying a big Underwood machine, partly braced against his grey apron, into the corner, where there was only a box with pieces of metal, bits of iron and other rubbish. Half-heartedly, but in a voice that was meant to be light and jocular, I asked him, "You're not going to throw this machine away, are you?"

"Yes," he said, looked at me, and put it on the counter for the moment. He was slight and perhaps even suffered a little from asthma or some other kind of ailment. At any rate he seemed pleased at the excuse to put the typewriter down again on his way to the rubbish corner. "It fell down earlier. Thank God it wasn't me but the boss. And the part on the right, which contains the spring which moves the carriage, snapped clean off. Broken, nothing more to be done." He wanted to pick the machine up again.

"Please wait a minute," I said. Then I asked what this machine cost. He called the boss, who came over too. "It's no use any more. What do you want with it?" "Oh, only for a child to play with," I lied. I got the machine for two shillings, a tenth of a pound sterling.

I almost gave out dragging it home, but I triumphed. I had my typewriter, and as good as new! Only the carriage didn't work. Once I had caught my breath, I left my room again, went to the nearest Woolworth's and for sixpence bought a stretch washing line made of rubber together with two hooks which fitted into the rings at the ends. Back home again, I put the machine on my table, fastened one ring to the left-hand side of the carriage, tugged at the washing line until it was fairly taut, then screwed a hook into the window frame and slipped on the loop. Back to the table! My invention worked! The flexible washing line pulled the carriage on by one letter at each stroke, just as the spring had originally done. Only the last three or four strokes in each line could not be used, then the tension relaxed too much.

My joy was hardly clouded by remembering only now that on my last outing, when I had bought the washing line, I had forgotten to buy typing paper and at least two or three sheets of carbon paper. That too was accomplished before the shops closed. In the evening I wrote the first ten or twelve pages and went to bed happy and satisfied. But I had bad dreams. I was in Vienna, in our apartment, from which we had been driven out, and I found my father in a dreadfully neglected room and in a wretched state, but still alive. I had to fetch our family doctor immediately, but was ashamed because of the disgustingly dirty room. When I did go to fetch him, without having taken the time to clean up, I woke up and for several seconds did not know whether my father was alive or dead.

The next morning the writing continued to go quite well although I became a little uneasy. The whole time, since my arrival in London, I knew, of course, that my father had died of the ill-treatment that he had suffered during an interrogation, and that my mother was still imprisoned in a Nazi gaol. But at least it had been clear to me that we were the innocent victims and that the Nazis, the destroyers of our family, the exterminators of the household into which I had been born eighteen years before, were to blame for everything. Now, in recording in precise detail all the accompanying circumstances, it was no longer all quite so simple.

True, the Nazis were still guilty. They were the exterminators, the destroyers, the murderers, but . . . Was there a but? Suddenly I was ravenously hungry and decided to take a walk down to the almost free canteen of the Refugee Committee in Fitzroy Square.

It was a long way, and when I had reached Fitzroy Square my hunger had grown even greater. Apart from that I was tired from walking and my feet were sore, for I had already worn the soles of my shoes down far too much and felt every bump in the pavement. Again I thought of Mr Berg's elegant shoes with their thick crepe soles.

Unusually, there was no queue of people outside the canteen waiting to gain admittance, so at least I would get in right away. But when I had reached the door I found it locked. A notice written with a fine flourish had been fixed to the door at about eye level. "After the distribution of 2,000 portions per day this canteen will be closed without fail until the following day."

Crushed, tired, dragging my feet, it was back to the north again, where I lived. On the way I bought myself a cold tough leathery steak and kidney pie for twopence halfpenny.

In my room I looked at the typewriter, and the keys looked at me. I was still happy to own my typewriter, but writing up the history of my family's destruction did not really seem to be getting any further. The charge against my father and against my mother had been: "Actions preparatory to the transfer of currency abroad." That was not a political offence, but broke financial regulations. And it also had apparently nothing to do with persecution by the Nazis. So a shameful lapse or crime? No. that was not a problem for me. A few sentences could explain it all truthfully. Elderly people, for example my grandmother, could not get a visa abroad at all without money, and apart from that, the major part of the money which my mother had tried to transfer abroad, even if in the clumsiest and most inexperienced manner imaginable, did not even belong to her, she had only quite unselfishly wanted to help other companions in misfortune.

But had it really been quite unselfish? Financially without a doubt. Mrs Markus, whose money above all was involved, was the cousin of the lawyer with whom my mother was on intimate terms. Yes, intimate. My parents' marriage had been like that for years, father and mother each going their own way. That too one would really have to write down exactly, if one wanted to get all the circumstances down on paper. Their own way, but not without constant arguing, which for years I had hardly been able to bear any more. That was only one of the reasons why I had longed to be grown up at last and escape this household. But how to explain all that?

Now I had escaped, and the household didn't exist any more, and my father was dead, and my hopes of getting my aged blind grandmother to England before the imminent outbreak of war with the help of the Refugee Committee, which postponed everything, sank from week to week.

Nevertheless that still had to be explained. So: My mother's friend, for whom she was terribly afraid, had refused to leave the country unless my mother undertook to save the Markus family's money. Not that my mother and Mrs Markus particularly liked one another. Mrs Markus had at some time been the lover of her cousin, Dr B. But my mother had no choice, if she wanted to make sure that Dr B. was safe.

My father had warned that it was too dangerous: "All this silly money business will end up getting us all into trouble!" But then it had been he who had found what seemed to be the way to save the money. An old wartime comrade, Hugo Marx, now practically a member of the Nazi Party, met by chance on the street and, as before, more than comradely, astonishingly helpful, had really got the money out of the frozen accounts. Easily explained. Jewish savings accounts were simply frozen at the time in Austria, but he was not a Jew and was a party member. It only came out later — in the course of the trial of my mother and Hugo Marx and of all the others who had flocked together as the news spread that there was a prospect of getting one's money out of the country — that he wanted to blackmail the account holders afterwards. Finally, on 24th April 1938, thirty men and women had sat down in the Café Thury, downstairs in the apartment block in which we lived, to discuss all the possibilities. Overheard by a waiter they had been denounced and promptly arrested.

All easily explained and therefore easy to write down too, but at that moment I couldn't write, for the more the memories crowded in and were followed by other memories, the more I had to weep and lost my self-control.

"I am the only one who knows all the connections. The others don't at all. You don't need to torment them with interrogations and you won't get anything out of me," my father had explained, upon which the officer in charge of the interrogation, Herr Göttler from Germany, had kicked in his intestinal wall. Had my father known that a refusal, expressed in these words, was suicide? Had he known that his wartime comrade Marx had already given everything away long before, and that Mrs Markus too, in a fit of hatred of my mother, mixed with the fear of death for herself, had long ago said everything she knew, which wasn't so little either?

Had my father really wanted to die, to look for a good brave exit, because he had had enough of his life, his marriage and his job? He saw everything as having gone wrong, as botched or wasted, as I had often heard him say late in the evening to his dog Piet, until a few months before, when Piet had died and my father had said, "I won't survive him by another year." This prediction too had now been fulfilled. Sitting in front of the new typewriter and weeping I remembered every one of my father's accusations against my mother and of my mother against my father and of my grandmother against both. Again and again they had said: "This mire," and whatever else I had had against their arguments, I had agreed with this word, for I too felt no differently and wanted to get out of this mire.

Now it was behind me, the mire. The only bit of mire that still surrounded me, was the description of the destruction of my family, for which I was to receive fifty pounds.

No, I didn't want to go on writing. It would end up looking as if my family and my family alone were to blame for their own destruction, and the Nazis had only been the executive organ of history, the *deus* or *diabolus ex machina*. And that could not be allowed. Not a word more!

But it still took more than another week before I was ready to write Mr Berg a short letter, saying that unfortunately I could not write the story of my family. I had borrowed a pound from a well-to-do refugee family, for I had already used up most of the other pound, and of course I had to enclose with the letter the two pounds which Mr Berg had provided for paper and small expenses. At that moment the fact that through this commission I had nevertheless come into possession of my new typewriter was no comfort to me.

Only much later did it become clear to me, that the failure of a marriage did not have to be the fault of one party or the other, as I had always assumed in the preceding years, and that mire had perhaps been too harsh an expression for a state which was already in itself very unpleasant, but which only became completely miserable because of the moralising and prejudices of everyone involved.

By the time I realised that, the war had already broken out and my grandmother had remained stuck in Vienna, and my mother had only just managed to reach England three days before the outbreak of war, and Mr Berg was no longer a successful, admired writer, but was called Peter Berg and I knew about his conflicts and fears too. And much later still he was a colleague, an exiled writer like myself, and later still he died, without having accomplished the works which were really closest to his heart.

Three Library Users

The narrow but tall house in Westbourne Terrace, W2, is well over a hundred years old. It was built in Queen Victoria's time and is still standing today, more than forty years after the three episodes to be described here.

The most diverse refugee organisations had established themselves all over London. By far the largest, the "Austrian Centre", with its youth organisation, "Young Austria," was here in Westbourne Terrace.

Offices, also a large meeting room for the left-wing core of the organisation. But the meeting room served also as a cabaret theatre and as a hall for larger events, and beneath it was a cheap restaurant for refugees, which however upheld the best traditions of Viennese cooking, and next to it, a single room, the small lending library.

I was the librarian. Behind my table, and to the right of it, two large bookcases, in front of me the cupboard with a few books to be repaired, which also contained the small amount of money for lending dues and replacement of lost books. On my table, card indexes and papers, warning letters to tardy borrowers, leaflets calling attention to meetings, and all kinds of odds and ends. Books too, of course, which I read when I happened to have a few free minutes.

The books were partly donated by refugees, partly contributed by the founders of the Austrian Centre themselves or bought new; the new books were mostly works by left-wing authors, which were supposed to expand the readers' horizons in this respect. The donated books in particular were of a diversity difficult to describe. Beside a few leather-bound volumes from the eighteenth century, there were more or less well-worn paperbacks from the Weimar Republic, then again fine, but very often incomplete editions of the classics; art nouveau books, art books, historical novels, philosophical treatises, essays, children's books, poetry and anthologies, and in among them old guide books and school books.

One day, shortly after the outbreak of war, while I was reading I was interrupted by a young woman. Her whole face was beaming. "Your system worked!" she called out to me, "I've got news from my mother! Very short only, a telegram. But news nevertheless!"

I was happy for her. The system she was talking about was a fairly simple one. A few weeks before the outbreak of war, I had organised a link via a country that would remain neutral, via Switzerland, that could pass on letters and telegrams. This news was the first case which proved that the link worked. "Only there's *one* word in the telegram I don't understand," said the young woman, "probably a greeting or something. My mother will have written it in German of course. But in Switzerland they translate it into English, and I don't understand enough English yet. Perhaps you can translate it for me?" She gave me the telegram. The word was "deceased" and the sentence had only three words: "Your mother deceased."

"Do sit down," I said. Then I tried to prepare her for the fact that the telegram was no cause for joy. At first she didn't understand, then she did not simply weep, but threw herself back and forward in a fit of sobbing, almost like a fish on dry land.

Forty-five years later, in another part of London, in Mill Lane, as I was rummaging through old books which were displayed outside a junk shop, I was asked by an old lady whether I was an Austrian poet. She said my name. When I answered, she said, "I'm sure you won't remember me any more, but I once brought you a telegram in the library of the Austrian Centre and asked you to translate it for me."

"Then you are Alice Zoldester," I said and she was surprised that I remembered. I would never have recognised her again, but how could I ever have forgotten that short translation?

*

At the outbreak of war, refugees from Germany and Austria were classified as "enemy aliens", which, depending on inclination, one could understand to mean "hostile foreigners" or "strangers from enemy countries". The description was an encouragement to mistrust. Very many refugee women, who earlier had received work permits only as servants, lost their jobs and were accommodated in hostels hastily organised by Bloomsbury House, the refugee committee. Apart from a bed and modest board they received sixpence a week pocket money, out of which they had to pay for travel, toiletries and similar things, which was of course impossible. Most of them sold or pawned their last pieces of jewellery or surplus clothes, but in almost every hostel there were one or two women who began to earn something extra by occasional prostitution. They then, of course, had far more money than the others, bought their room-mates chocolate, cigarettes or eau de cologne and said to one or other of the young girls, "Go on, come along to the coffee house and take a look for yourself. You don't have to go with anyone you don't like." One such girl who came along was Ruth, a member of "Young Austria," and a fairly enthusiastic reader in my lending library, beautiful, tall, dark-haired.

When it somehow became known in Young Austria, our youth organisation, that she, as the group leader said, "had gone astray," it was decided to expel her for "un-Austrian be-haviour". Ruth came into the library weeping, told me about it, and I intervened.

"First, if we have created a youth organisation, in order to influence these people politically," I said, "then we also have the duty, as a youth organisation, to take care of members who have got into difficulties and not throw them out. Second, given the living conditions of these girls and women in their hostels it's no surprise at all. It's more a surprise that many more don't go astray. And third, it's far from being un-Austrian behaviour! Since the beginning of the depression it's not been so unusual at home either. Has it?"

The decision was overturned, Ruth came back to the library

to thank me. A girl in the group was to talk to her and take care of her. For a few weeks she really did come regularly to the group evenings and members' meetings again. Then, one evening, she turned up in the library to bring back some books. "No, I don't want any new ones. I want to thank you once again for having tried to help me, but I won't come again. It's really no use. Most of them ignore me or look at me with contempt or try to sleep with me as fast as they can. Or both at the same time, in that they ignore me in the group but afterwards try to get off with me. I can't bear it any more, I'm not coming back."

My arguments had no effect. My suggestion, just to come to me if she needed anything, was also rejected with a shake of the head. At the last moment, before she went out, she gave me a kiss on the forehead and was gone before I could recover from my astonishment. Only the smell of her perfume remained for a few seconds.

Years later I read her name in the newspaper. Her skull had been identified from dental work. She had been killed by Christie, the mentally disturbed London murderer who could not be tender to living women, and had been buried in his house at Notting Hill Gate about a week later.

One day about three years before the end of the war, money began to go missing from the little box in the library cupboard. It was repeated when I stuck a note to the little box, please not to take any money out of it, but to get in touch with me, if there were problems or need. Finally I left only a couple of small coins in the little box, so that it still rattled, and painted it with silver nitrate, which turns fingers indelibly black for days if touched. Three days later the thief had already betrayed himself in this way. It was Fred, a member of Young Austria, eighteen or nineteen years old. I had occasionally asked him to look after the library just for a few minutes, when I had to leave the room.

He began to cry at my further questioning. Yes, he had also taken something else. Among other things, he had robbed the rent, gas and electricity cash box in a communal flat in which he was staying. In total the sum made up a much larger amount than I would have imagined. Enough to live on for months.

"For heaven's sake, why did you do it? You've got a job! Are you not earning enough?" I knew that Young Austria had decided that all members had to work in factories or join the army, in order to support the defence of the Soviet Union and contribute their share to the victory over Hitler. Miserably Fred said, that was just it, because in reality he didn't have any work. He had indeed gone to the factory at first, but frequently come too late and had been dismissed. He had not dared report it to the group leadership and at the communal flat pretended he was going to work every morning. But then during the day, in order not to be spotted, he had hidden away in cinemas and seen the same film three or four times in a row. Fred was actually relieved that the truth had come out and this double life was now at an end.

He registered voluntarily for military service and promised to pay back his debts. What he had taken from the library cash box was trifling and I replaced it. Perhaps I had a bad conscience because I had caught him. Once he even visited me in uniform in the library and was very pleased when I again left the cash box in his care, because I had to discuss something in an office upstairs for a couple of minutes.

I have never found out whether Fred survived the war or not. I had only been able to help him a little bit more than Ruth or Alice, who had come into the library with the telegram from her mother, full of joy and gratitude because the link via Switzerland had worked. In any case, that was the only occasion on which the connection ever really did work.

Läzchen

I dreamt about him for the first time in forty years, about him and about Eva. Not only dreamt, because in the dream it occurred to me, for the first time, that his name Lazar was really an abbreviation of Lazarus. And of course I dreamt too, that I said, "Arise and walk." But I was not Jesus of Nazareth and Herbert Lazar was not Lazarus in the Gospels, and a dream is not a miracle, or at least works no miracles, and so no one walked, and after waking up I was a little confused for ten or twenty seconds. Not even as many seconds, as years have passed since then.

We never called him Herbert or even Lazar, but always Läzchen. He was Viennese like me, but most of us were from Germany, hence the German diminutive form Läzchen. He was about the same age as I was, eighteen or nineteen, and someone — I don't know any more whether it was Max or Anni or Gerti — had brought him along to our small circle of young German and Austrian refugees which at that time, in spring 1940, met once or twice a week in West Hampstead, London. We tried to help one another, to find work for each other, also addresses in neutral countries through which we wanted to make contact with our family and friends who had remained stranded in Hitler's Reich. We discussed possibilities of escape for them and job possibilities for us and occasionally helped one another to find accommodation. This was not easy, because although refugees, since the outbreak of war we were officially registered as "enemy aliens" which seemed far too suspect to many English landlords for them to go on tolerating such people in their homes or take them in, especially now that France was just collapsing.

Stephan and I shared an attic room at number 67 Priory

Road, West Hampstead, and things were going well for us, even if only thanks to a misunderstanding on the part of our landlord, a man who very much enjoyed a drink, which then made him especially jovial. The Sneeds were about fifty, he was a lawyer and always came home late. She, it is true, enjoyed a drink not much less than he did, but tirelessly busied herself around the house, her appearance and character not unlike an intelligent, nimble grey rat.

One evening Mr Sneed had called my friend Stephan and myself into the parlour. He had invited us to sit down with them by the fireside, which was in reality only an electric radiator, but in the fashion of the time it was embellished with transparent yellow and red coals made of some kind of plastic, behind which, with the help of the glowing elements, an ingenious clockwork set in motion by the heat was supposed to create the impression of a glowing fire. We had to drink a glass of port with Mr and Mrs Sneed, then Mr Sneed stood up, cleared his throat and informed us, that in this house we should not worry in the least about this sudden aversion to enemy aliens. To him we were simply Germans, and the Germans were the natural allies of the English — ''Heil Hitler!'' With that we were graciously dismissed. To put him right would have had as a consequence the immediate loss of our room.

The cordiality of the Sneeds made it possible for us to hold the meetings of our little circle undisturbed in Priory Road, although Mrs Sneed was really by nature a fairly strict landlady.

To one of these meetings there then also came Läzchen, a friendly, slim, brown haired boy, good-natured, very short-sighted, with conspicuously thick spectacle lenses. Unlike most of the others, however, he could not come regularly because he didn't live in London but down in Kent, near the coast, in the so-called Kitchener Camp at Sandwich. Kitchener Camp was an old military camp, which had supposedly been built at one time by Lord Kitchener. It had already been put at the disposal of the Jewish Refugee Committee some time before the war, and those German and Austrian refugees for whom the committee had found neither work nor lodgings were accommodated there.

They lived in comfortable barracks, the food was good too, but they were not allowed to leave the camp without permission. In reality they had long ago dug secret tunnels under the perimeter fence in several places, through which they could slip in or out whenever they wished, to meet girls from Richborough or Sandwich or to get a lift to London from passing cars and look for work and accommodation there. They could even smuggle guests, who were also fed there, into the camp along the narrow passageways, but the men, some of whom had come out of concentration camps only just before their journey to England and who now found themselves in a camp again, complained. Some of the more embittered went so far as to claim that Kitchener Camp was worse than Dachau, and also that the food was worse than in a concentration camp, which was of course not true. At Läzchen's invitation, and also to see how the people there lived, I had spent a week in the camp myself, just before the outbreak of war, as a secretly infiltrated guest, and never ever, since I had to leave Vienna, eaten so well.

Läzchen too was now looking around in London for a place to stay and trying to trace relatives, which he finally succeeded in doing.

One evening, when he had still not found his relatives, he wanted to go out again, to visit someone, but because, as an "enemy alien," he was not allowed to be on the streets after midnight and it was impossible for him to get back to Kitchener Camp the same evening, we had agreed to let him secretly stay the night with us. Our landlady would never have allowed it. He was to whistle outside our window when he returned. It would have been better to lend him a key, but we were still too inexperienced for that to occur to us. Instead we had agreed on a rather complicated whistle and practised it together.

It was fairly late before Läzchen finally whistled. I ran to the door, but to my horror Läzchen was not alone in the front garden. Short-sighted and clumsy as he was he had not noticed, but a few steps behind him stood a silent observer, a policeman whose attention he had evidently drawn because of his whistling and his foreign clothing.

When I had opened the door and greeted Läzchen, the policeman stepped forward. "Does this young man live here?"

"Yes, of course," I said.

"No, of course not," contradicted Mrs Sneed, who had also come to the door, without my having noticed. "I have never seen him before."

The policeman thanked her. Then, turning to Läzchen, "Come with me to the police station." Läzchen, without a word, made to follow him.

"Just a moment," I said. "I'll just pull on my coat and come with you. I think I can clear the matter up. If anyone is to blame, then I am."

The policeman waited. With a heavy heart, I closed the door behind me, and we got going along Priory Road towards Broadhurst Gardens. The police station was not very far at all, round the corner after the next, in West End Lane.

"You know very well that you are not allowed to stay the night without notification," the policeman said to Läzchen. It was something between a statement and a question.

I broke in. "I'm not certain, if he knows the rules so well. I had offered to let him stay the night with us. And I thought it was only that one was not allowed to be on the streets after midnight. And in any case, do take the human side of the matter into account!" I began to explain Läzchen's situation as a refugee from Hitler and the urgent necessity of finding work and accommodation, since it was an open secret that those remaining in Kitchener Camp, which was far too near the coast, would probably be interned very soon to get them away from there.

The policeman stopped and looked at us. "To tell you the truth, I am Jewish myself too. I know very well that this classification as 'hostile aliens' is nonsense and an injustice. We shall see what can be done."

Meanwhile we had arrived in West End Lane. The blue lamp of the police station appeared in front of us, even though it was almost completely dimmed because of the blackout, but to our astonishment the policeman walked on. "Come with me."

We walked down West End Lane, and immediately after the

police station crossed West Hampstead Mews on the left, then Compayne Gardens, Cleve Road and Woodchurch Road. Not until the next side street, Acol Road, did we turn left and then left again, into Priory Road, back to our house. The policeman rang and Mrs Sneed opened the front door.

"We have been to the police station," said the policeman, "and have looked into the matter. It would be best if on this occasion the young man could spend the night with you. We can also pay, whatever needs to be paid."

"No, no. It's a pleasure for me, to be able to help!" she insisted, suddenly overflowing with friendliness again. "If *you* say so, and after all, if it's a friend of our tenant!" We said goodbye to the policeman, whom we could not even thank as we really wanted to, because Mrs Sneed remained within earshot.

That saved Läzchen from the internment that would have been certain, if the matter really had got as far as the police station, and I know that I was a little proud of my speech, which had prevented it. Läzchen did manage to find his relatives the next day and stayed with them. From then on he attended our meetings regularly for about two months. We argued fiercely. Unlike the rest of us, Läzchen was a convinced Zionist, though a follower of Martin Buber, who did not want to eject the Palestinians or treat them as second-class citizens, but believed in equality and fraternity. We tried to explain to him that it was an illusion, and in reality the Palestinians would certainly suffer.

"No! I shall prove the opposite to you! I am going there next week!" Läzchen triumphantly revealed to us one evening. He had obtained a place on a freighter illegally taking Jews to Palestine and was overjoyed. Although politically we did not share his viewpoint, we wished him all the best and because we all liked him, asked him to write to us at length.

No letter came from him. Nothing. But we were not too surprised at his silence, because sudden departure for completely new surroundings often means that one loses touch with old acquaintances.

One or two months later our little group was itself scattered by the accidents of war. Only years later did I hear by chance what had happened to Läzchen. It would have been better for him if I had said nothing to the policeman and if Läzchen had been interned.

The freighter was unlucky. The ship, a pitiful old crate, a real floating coffin, was intercepted by the English shortly before landing, and the passengers only reached Palestine after many months internment in Cyprus. All except one, Läzchen. He had had the misfortune to break his glasses on board. But without his glasses the shortsighted boy was as good as blind, which made him even more uncertain and clumsy. When the English had intercepted the boat and English soldiers came on board, one of them ordered, "Everyone, move back there!" Everyone fell back, only the boy deprived of his glasses promptly set out in the wrong direction. "Move back there, or I'll fire!" shouted the soldier once again. When Läzchen blindly went on, he fired.

Läzchen died in the arms of a girl who had fallen in love with him on the freighter. The English soldier bent down helplessly over him. Läzchen's last words were: "It was not his fault. I went in the wrong direction. Sorry."

The girl was called Eva Tannenbaum and was very beautiful. She did not feel happy in Palestine and still less so in independent Israel, because she did not like the way the Palestinians were treated by the settlers and immigrants. She came to England, where I got to know her by chance. Later she married a mathematician from New York and a few years later in America took her own life together with that of her child.

When one grows older than they did, the dead sometimes turn up unexpectedly, in a chance memory, or at night in a dream. But they do not arise and they do not walk.

Fini

When I was a child, the so-called respectable children still had a nurse maid, a children's maid, or, as we called it, a children's miss. My favourite children's miss was called Fini and had blonde hair. Her real name was Josephine Freisler, and she was one of three daughters of a country doctor in Gaaden near Vienna, who, however, had been ill for a long time and could no longer support his family properly.

Although Fini got on well with my grandmother, she was nevertheless occasionally a refuge from the latter's anger, as only our dogs were otherwise. I don't think that I loved Fini much less than my grandmother. I loved her long blonde hair which I liked to comb and brush, I loved her voice, whether she was speaking or singing songs. I loved everything about her, her appearance, her smell, the way she moved. But above all, perhaps, I loved her nature. She was the most sincere and kind-hearted person whom I had got to know until then.

When, at the age of five, I appeared on stage in and around Vienna, certified as a child wonder and spoiled by the public with chocolate and flowers, Fini always came to the rehearsals and performances. It was she who took me there and brought me home again afterwards. My mother and my grandmother only came to the performances themselves, especially to the first nights.

The theatre milieu was not without an effect on Fini. One day I was in the room, when she explained to my grandmother that it was her greatest wish to become an actress. After some reflection, my grandmother said she could certainly attend an acting course, preferably while I was at school, which I was due to start at the end of the summer, for I had now reached school age. But in the evenings, said my grandmother, Fini must devote herself to me, and put me to bed, read me fairy tales and do everything else that was necessary.

Fini became lost in thought, as to whether her courses could be made to fit in with her duties to me. But once my grandmother was out of the room, I ran to her, put my arm around her shoulder and said: "I can go to bed all by myself. And if I want to have fairy tales, I can read them all by myself too. But I think we can do it so that you sit beside my bed in the evening and read your parts out to me. If it's possible, I can read them along with you and check whether you have learned your parts and whether you are pronouncing the words properly." At first Fini thought this suggestion was only a kind of pipe dream, but I assured her again and again, in the end almost with impatience, that I meant it seriously and really wanted to do it. Finally she embraced and kissed me and consented. She said nothing to my grandmother about our agreement, because I had explicitly forbidden her to do so.

In the next two years she attended her drama courses while I was at school. In the evenings we proceeded as we had agreed. Everything went wonderfully, the only difficult thing during this time was that she had to have her long blonde hair cut off, in order to play certain roles. I cried so long about it, that she began to cry too. After about two years her course was over. It was followed by a short full-time probationary period, and then Fini was an actress. I refused to have another children's miss after her.

In some respects those were probably the best years of my childhood. Every day, I looked forward to the evenings with Fini, and in the school holidays she took me with her to the family home in Gaaden, where the old cat, called "the pensioner", woke me up every morning by licking my face with her rough tongue. Sometimes, however, to the dismay of Fini and myself, she brought a dead bird to my bed, which she presumably wanted to present to me as nourishment.

In Fini's house there were quite different books and calendars than at home, but despite that I did not like to stay long in the living room, because the two fly traps hanging from the lamp, long sticky strips of fly paper, on which countless flies and a few moths and butterflies were slowly dying, distressed me. Fini too could not bear these instruments of martyrdom easily, but her mother insisted on using them.

Behind the house, however, waited the big, overgrown meadow with tall grass and flowers and overrun with weeds, which stretched down to the brook. At the brook one could play with the local children, build dams, dig side-channels and splash around as much as one wanted. In the neighbouring property there were even hens running around, which was so interesting that I went there again and again, even though I had once or twice found a dead chick crawling with maggots.

Shortly after Fini was offered her first role, she had to leave Vienna because it was not a Viennese theatre in which she was to act. She still read this part out to me, in memory of our evenings, as if she was still dependent on my correction of her pronunciation.

Fini continued to visit from time to time, but finally she became engaged to a Mr Eckelmann who lived in Germany, in Dresden or Leipzig. As a small child I had always declared I would marry her, once I was big enough, and something of these fantasies had evidently stayed with me, because when she married, I cried for a long time, although she wrote me a card, saying that she would never forget me. I believe I was never so jealous again.

The years passed, Hitler came, my exile in England, then the war. I had lost all trace of Fini.

Not until 1950 or 1951, when I had begun to read reflections and short stories on the radio, did I hear from her again. She had survived the war, was now in the East, herself had children, already grown up, was once more working as an actress and had been extremely happy to hear me on the radio. For some reason she had thought I and my whole family had been killed by the Nazis. I wrote a long letter, told her about myself, that I too had a child, and about which of my family had died and who had survived. With one of her subsequent letters Fini sent me a childhood photograph that shows me at the time when she was my children's miss. It is the only childhood photo of myself that I still have.

She also wrote that she still remembered the evenings on which I went through the parts with her, and that she had never known another child that had behaved even remotely like me. Despite my request, Fini did not send me a picture of herself, or perhaps it got lost in the post.

I wrote my broadcasts to the GDR, and read them into the microphone, in the German-language service of the BBC. Since at that time the Stalin era was not yet over, and I had been disappointed by Stalinism, I also had harsh words for conditions in the East. After Stalin's death, I did not, it is true, adopt the Cold War rhetoric of other radio commentators, but was nevertheless for a while *persona non grata* in the GDR and for about three years was not even allowed to set foot in the part of Berlin belonging to the GDR.

During this time I had dropped our correspondence, in order not to cause any possible problems for Fini. But around this time also, there was a serious break-in at our house, as a result of which a large number of papers went missing, including Fini's address. I must still have had one or two letters from Fini, but could not find them again in the mountains of my old papers.

When I was allowed to step on GDR territory once more, I tried to find out Fini's address, but without any luck — even when I once spent a few days in the GDR. I think I will never stop asking myself why my attempts at the time were not more determined. I would have had no lack of opportunities. Perhaps I was somehow afraid of seeing a Fini who had aged. Perhaps it was also a faintheartedness in salvaging something from the great loss of my childhood and adolescence brought about by Hitlerism, that made me fail. Because it was a failure.

At the time I was hoping that my next stay in the GDR would be a longer one, but whenever one was planned, nothing came of it because I fell dangerously ill. Not until spring 1986 did I actually get as far as setting out on my eagerly anticipated reading tour of the GDR. I read in Dresden, in Leipzig and in Berlin. Everything was even better than I had expected, and the infinitely helpful editor at my GDR publishers, whose kind-heartedness and sincerity reminded me again and again of Fini, tried desperately to track Fini down. There were private enquiries and a directory of GDR actors too, but it was all no use. Presumably the search also failed, because I was only looking for Fini under her married name.

The thought that I was perhaps not very far from her at all, but in the end unable to see her again, was more tormenting than I could have imagined possible when I was far away, in England, where I lived, or even in Hamburg or Vienna.

On one of the days of my reading tour I was to be interviewed for GDR television. Immediately after being introduced, the interviewer, a young man, said, "A question before we begin the interview: Does the name Josephine Freisler mean anything to you?"

I almost jumped out of my seat. "Does it mean anything to me!" Josephine Freisler. Fini, my old children's miss! I've been looking everywhere for her for days! Where is she?"

"I can't say exactly, but ten years ago when I was just starting out, she was acting at the theatre in Senftenberg. Things weren't going very well for me at the time, and she helped me more than anyone else. She was already an old lady, and she was unbelievably kind-hearted and understanding and quite different from the other actors. And she was always talking about you."

Only now had Fini really come tangibly close to me. My editor phoned the theatre in Senftenberg the very same day, but only reached the director the following day. The latter remembered Fini very well and also knew her address, even though she had not been performing any more for years. Fini did not have a telephone, but the director was prepared to drive out at the weekend and look her up. Mrs Freisler, she said, must indeed be rather old, but had always lived very healthily and had always been robust. She would certainly still be there.

My editor also asked the director to pass on greetings from me, and a promise that I would write in a few days. My GDR visa ran out too soon for me to visit Fini this time, but my editor and I discussed whether we could not get it extended. Otherwise I would without doubt come again soon. Meanwhile I had also written a letter to Fini, which I gave to the editor, until we received some news. I also included a thousand marks from my GDR fees as a present for her.

But then the director could not go at the weekend after all, only the following day. She had too much to do. And I had to leave the GDR before that.

On the day after my departure I called my editor up. She had received news from the director. Fini had died six months earlier.

Comfort

A little while ago in a junk shop in South London I found a damaged book that I did not need at all. I bought it because it was old and cheap and I felt sorry for it. At home I stuck it together and looked at it more closely. It was *The Book of Common Prayer*, the Anglican prayer book, an early eighteenth-century edition, beautifully printed and a good four times as thick as the newer editions with exactly the same text. At both front and back there were three blank pages and on them I found a wealth of names and dates, some in fancy and shaky handwriting and others again in very simple, sensitive and yet firm handwriting (sometimes interrupted by clumsy, hardly legible or partly deleted entries). The surnames were almost always the same, except sometimes the women's. The dates referred to birth and death, baptism, wedding, military service by family members, or to their emigration. Whose property the prayer book was at any one time, was also conscientiously recorded.

In such a book one expects after a date of birth the entry of the death of the person concerned to follow after an appropriate interval. So it was here too. But there was one family with many children, in which each child had died after a few weeks or months. The deciphering of these old notes upset me all the more, perhaps, because I already had children and grandchildren of my own. Only a single child, a girl, had apparently escaped death and only her date of birth was entered; however, I found neither confirmation nor wedding. Nevertheless, she seemed to have remained alive. But a few weeks later, when I showed the book to friends, we also discovered on a page somewhere in the middle of the book a note of her death after all:

". . . departed this world at the age of two years nine and a half months." I was disappointed and quite unreasonably sad. When I tried to console myself with the thought that more than two hundred years had passed, and she could not be alive any more anyway, I remembered my own childhood.

I was a sheltered child. Except if my parents happened to be having an argument, during which occasionally all kinds of unbearable things were mentioned, nothing was said to me about the hardships of life and death. When I found a very detailed pictorial representation of the martyrdom of Christians in a Roman arena, I was first of all fobbed off with the words, "But those are just very old stories. It's not perhaps even true." And then, when I evidently could not be dissuaded of the truth of the persecution of the Christians and in tears pointed at the individual youths, women and children, I was consoled with the thought, "But after all, they couldn't be alive any more anyway."

It was my grandmother who said that to me and who in the first years of childhood played the largest part in my upbringing. This time I was immediately persuaded of the truth of her argument, and even if I felt that it was only a sad comfort, my tears did begin to dry up.

One or two years later my grandmother showed me a very old photograph, the yellowed portrait of a very young man in an old-fashioned uniform. It was one of her relations, who was part of her earliest childhood memories. He had let her ride on his knees, but had been killed, when she was still less than three years old, in 1866 in Bohemia, during the Austro-Prussian War. She told me how he had been shot. He had refused to let himself be taken prisoner. "An Austrian does not surrender!" he had shouted.

When I saw that my grandmother's face was sad, I tried to make use of her old words of comfort, stroked her arm as she had stroked mine, and said, with an emphasis as close as possible to the one with which she had said it to me: "But after all, he couldn't be alive any more anyway."

My grandmother protested, "Oh yes, of course he could still

be alive!" At the same time, however, she began to calculate under her breath with the help of her fingers. Finally she said, "I don't know, I think he could still be alive. He would not yet be eighty years old."

Since I knew that at thirty one is *old*, eighty was an almost inconceivably great age. No one in our family had reached it. In the end my grandmother did not reach it either. At seventy-nine she was taken from the Theresienstadt ghetto to an extermination camp and gassed there. Right until the end of the Second World War I had still hoped to see her alive again. She would have been almost eighty-one.

I found it hard to comfort myself about her death. Even now, I have only re-read a very few of her last letters, which she wrote before her deportation, because even after all these years, I always started crying so much, even at the first lines, that I could not go on reading and pushed them back into the box with the label Grandmama. But in the last twenty years the pain on thinking of my grandmother has become less. Almost no one lives to be a hundred, so she couldn't be alive any more anyway.

I also say that to myself now, at the memory of my father's death. He died five years before my grandmother, exactly on his forty-eighth birthday. When he was brought home at midday of the day on which he died, I met him as he was being dragged up the stairs, and did not recognise him at first, but thought, when I saw our neighbour beside the wheezing old man, that he was somehow with her, and that the policeman and the driver who were lifting this dying man from step to step, only had something to do with her, nothing to do with me and my grandmother. I still remember my relief about it. When I asked our neighbour, who had evidently already spoken to the two men, and now accompanied them weeping, whether I could help her in any way, she seized me by the arm and said, "Don't you know who that is? That is your father!"

A Gestapo official, Mr Göttler, later a customs official in Düsseldorf, in West Germany, had kicked in his stomach wall a few days before.

Perhaps it had been the white stubble which had prevented

me from recognising my father at first sight on the darkened stairs. I had never seen him other than clean shaven. And that last time, the day of his arrest, exactly one month before his death, he had still no grey or even white hairs. Then when I saw him again, three days after his death, in the open coffin, he had been shaved and looked somewhat better, as if death had meant a rest for him.

Then the war came soon after. — Today my father would be ninety-eight years old. So presumably he couldn't be alive any more anyway.

If war comes again, it will be a nuclear war. I ask myself whether here in Europe the survival of the survivors, wherever the survivors may be, will be such that they will still be able to mourn other people at all. If yes, then perhaps a few decades later it will again be said, first about those who were already old when they died, then somewhat later about the young and finally about the children too: "But now they couldn't be alive any more anyway." Only, whether it will still be said in German, whether German will still be a living language then, is the question.

Perhaps those who will talk about the dead then, will be people from another continent; or perhaps only after a very long time will they live in the place, where at the end of our time there was a war. Then it is possible that they will not only say, the dead of those days would have died a long time ago anyway, but apart from that they will also say, at least to their children, as comfort: "But those are just very old stories. It's perhaps not even true."

Sometimes, while thinking about it all, I suffer less from fear of death (although I am also not free of this fear, but more as a fear for my children and grandchildren) than from the feeling that I myself am infinitely, indeed unbearably old, so that at such moments I am only with an effort able to resist the thought, I may not now be alive any more anyway.